Why didn't he just take her in his arms?

The sight of him and the memory of the intimacies they had shared the night before made her shy of him. "I'm starting the book." Jessica waved at the pile of papers and books in front of her. "And I have to do more interviews, lunch with Daniel, sign a contract...." She was rattling on and on! Why didn't Philip stop her?

But he just turned away, saying, "You sound very busy. I won't keep you."

Uncertainty held Jessica in place. This Philip was reminiscent of the man she had married—cool and aloof, his thoughts a mystery, his emotions masked and frightening.

The same feelings of vulnerability and inadequacy that had plagued Jessica throughout her marriage stopped her from taking that step toward him...and reconciliation.

Books by Claire Harrison

These books may be available at your local bookseller.

For a list of all titles currently available,
send your name and address to:

Harlequin Reader Service
P.O. Box 52040, Phoenix, AZ 85072-2040
Canadian address: P.O. Box 2800, Postal Station A,
5170 Yonge St., Willowdale, Ont. M2N 5T5

CLAIRE HARRISON

once a lover

Harlequin Books

TORONTO • NEW YORK • LONDON
AMSTERDAM • PARIS • SYDNEY • HAMBURG
STOCKHOLM • ATHENS • TOKYO • MILAN

Harlequin Presents first edition November 1984
ISBN 0-373-10736-6

Original hardcover edition published in 1984
by Mills & Boon Limited

CHAPTER ONE

THE television taping was going well and Jessica made the fatal error of being lulled into relaxation. The grey suede chair in the station was comfortable, the camera was less obtrusive than usual, the kleig lights didn't shine directly into her eyes and the interviewer was displaying an unusual amount of charm, wit and intelligence. She could have sworn, during certain parts of her cross-country publicity tour, that most television stations hired hosts far more for their polished good looks than for their brain power.

This interviewer was different, however. He might have the usual combination of well-groomed dark hair and smooth smile, but he had an earnest boyishness that was appealing and it was quite apparent that he'd read both her books and knew them thoroughly. Most interviewers Jessica had come across had either skimmed her books or not read them at all, an act of negligence that invariably came to light when they opened their mouths and asked stupid questions. She'd become so accustomed to rehashing her own work and explaining what she had done that she'd never quite realised how pleasant it was to talk to someone who could go beyond the basics and discuss the material in depth.

'I found both your books fascinating, Miss Harley,' he was saying, 'and *Lost Souls: Battered Wives in America* was especially poignant. Did you find it difficult to interview those women?'

Jessica swivelled slightly in her chair so that she could face him more directly. 'Sometimes I felt like crying,' she admitted; 'and sometimes I felt furiously angry. The women were so unhappy, so desperate and so helpless.'

'Did you feel like a crusader when you wrote this book?'

'I couldn't change the system,' she said slowly, 'and I couldn't materially help women who had left their husbands, but I did come to feel that I was speaking on their behalf, that I was presenting their case to the public.'

'There has been some criticism that the book is one-sided, and that the stories of the husbands have been left out. Do you feel that's justified?'

Jessica unconsciously lifted one hand and smoothed back a tendril of black hair that had come loose from her chignon. Of course, she'd read the reviews of her books and knew that certain critics had felt that her case histories of beaten wives were not complete because she had neglected to interview the husbands, but she had her own defence ready.

'Physical violence is never justified,' she replied softly. 'It doesn't matter how irate a man becomes, he has no right to hit a woman who cannot defend herself.'

The interviewer deftly changed the direction of he conversation. 'And *All's Fair: The Battle Between the Sexes* —how did you feel about talking to those women and their stories of divorces and separations?'

He lifted the book up towards the camera lens so the audience-to-be would see its cover and Jessica winced inwardly. She hated the cover art on her latest book. She'd fought her publisher over it and lost to the overwhelming vote of the sales force who thought that a pink mushroom cloud on electric blue would sell better than a more dignified abstract design in toned-down colours.

'I guess sad is the word I would use,' she said. 'Their lives had been altered, some quite abruptly, and most of them didn't have either the emotional or financial means to support themselves. Some were in their forties and fifties and had never worked at all; they were lost without their husbands and often had little experience in dealing with the outside world.'

'The title implies that divorce is a battle of both sexes, yet again you left out stories about the husbands. Was that deliberate?'

'I'm afraid the title was chosen by the publisher,' she replied. 'They thought it was catchy. I really wanted to tell the story of women who'd been left high and dry when their husbands divorced them.'

The interviewer leaned back in his chair and gave her an understanding smile as if he too had had the experience of being packaged and polished for the sole purpose of being sold to the public. 'How did you get into the business of telling the stories of bereft women?'

This was good, solid ground upon which Jessica felt very comfortable. 'I have a college degree in sociology,' she explained, 'and I wanted to write. I began free-lancing after graduation and found that I enjoyed writing about women's issues for magazines like *McCall's* and *Redbook*. Both books are really expansions of themes that I've worked on before.'

'Is it exciting to have a book on the bestseller list?'

Jessica made a self-deprecating gesture. 'It's unexpected,' she said. 'I hadn't thought that I'd arouse so much controversy.'

'You made some strong statements in *All's Fair* about the way men act,' he said. 'In fact, its basic thesis is that we're really no better than our cave-man ancestors, only somewhat more civilized. Isn't that rather harsh, Miss Harley?'

His voice was interested and and calm as if he intended to keep the discussion on an abstract plane, and Jessica gave a sigh of relief. Some of her male interviewers had been overtly hostile, angry at the statements she had made in her book and intent upon cutting her down to size. This one seemed more open-minded and less ready to take everything she said in a personal vein.

'The longer I interviewed women,' she explained, 'the more convinced I became that the rising divorce rate is symptomatic of men's desire to get out of their commitments.'

'Are you saying that some wives don't leave their husbands?'

Jessica had handled that question before. 'No,' she said, 'but the reverse seems to be far more prevalent. A good number of the women I spoke to had husbands who had left them for younger women. They wanted their marriages to last; their husbands obviously didn't.'

The interviewer nodded sagely. 'Basically you're saying that divorce has become less of a stigma now and men are taking advantage of it.'

Jessica reluctantly inclined her head. 'That's how it looks to me.'

'Did any personal experience play a part in your books, Miss Harley?'

Only a small warning bell went off in Jessica's mind. Everything had been going along so smoothly. The interviewer had seemed so compassionate and sympathetic; he positively gave off an aura of understanding. Of course, she had known that he was good; the show was being taped in New York and it was one of the more sophisticated interview formats in the country. The publicity department in the publishing house had been ecstatic at getting her booked with him, and Jessica had counted herself lucky that his was the last interview of her tour rather than the first, knowing that she'd need the poise she had gained to face him.

'Personal experience?' she asked, seeking time to think.

'You're divorced, aren't you, Miss Harley?'

He was still smiling but this time Jessica could see the predator behind those very white teeth and she realised just how adept he had been at leading her up to this question.

She hoped that her clenched hands wouldn't show on the camera. 'Yes,' she said, her voice deceptively calm.

There was a brief silence while they looked at one another; the interviewer suddenly irritated under his air of glossy charm, Jessica now very wary behind her public face. She fell back on the experience of a hundred interviews, knowing that she did not have to amplify her answer, that she did not have to keep the conversational ball rolling and that, occasionally, a blunt response forced the interviewer to change direction—leading away from a dangerous line of enquiry.

Unfortunately, this interviewer was also far more experienced than many she had met, and persistent as well. 'Did your husband leave you?' he asked.

'It was a mutual parting of the ways.'

'Weren't you married to Philip Masters, the race-car driver?'

Jessica shifted uncomfortably. 'Yes.'

The interviewer suddenly leaned forward, moving in for the kill. 'Did he beat you, Miss Harley?'

'No.' She kept smiling while she wished for a knife to put between those curious, clever eyes. She'd learned quite early in her career as an author that anger, loosed from its usual restraints, could be dangerous. She'd been caught unawares during her first few brushes with the media and had revealed far more about herself than she had intended.

'I can't help feeling,' he said conversationally, 'that there's a bias in your work against men that must come from something deeper than your sympathy for other women. An antipathy, perhaps? A dislike of men?'

Jessica was already bathed in sweat, but none of her nervousness showed on the patrician lines of her face. 'Don't be silly,' she said lightly. 'Some of my best friends are men.'

'Darling, you look like you could use a stiff drink!'

Jessica laughed as Megan hugged her and closed the front door of her apartment behind them. 'It's a little early for that, isn't it?'

'Was the interview as bad as you look?'

'Worse,' Jessica conceded wryly. 'The hardest I've been through yet.'

'Well, sit down and relax. How long are you staying?'

Jessica allowed herself to be led into Megan's living room. 'Not long. I'm leaving on the shuttle this afternoon.'

Megan's expressive mouth turned down at the corners. 'Simon and I hoped you'd be staying for a while.'

'I'd love to,' Jessica said with a sigh, 'but I have to go back to work.'

Megan shook her finger at Jessica. 'All work and no play will make you exceedingly dull. Now, sit down, put your feet up and I'll get you something non-alcoholic but refreshing.'

'That sounds nice,' Jessica said as Megan retreated into the kitchen.

She pulled off her coat, slipped off the jacket to her navy suit and kicked off her shoes, letting her stockinged feet sink into the carpet and breathing a sigh of relief as she sat down on Megan's plump leather sofa. The rest of the interview had been anti-climactic after the personal questions and had even ended on a pleasant note; but Jessica was utterly thankful that she had finished her tour. She was tired of travelling, of sitting on planes, waiting at airports and living out of a suitcase. She hadn't actually been quite truthful with Megan. She didn't have to begin work right away; her next book could wait, but much as she enjoyed visiting the Thompsons she needed peace and the quiet solitude of her home.

She glanced out of the window that lined one wall of Megan's living room and made a face at the dreary, grey sky and jagged line of skyscrapers. She liked to visit New York, but she always found it exhausting. And it was never at its best in March, the city was damp and bleak and a cold wind seemed to blow around every corner. Jessica was looking forward to her return to Washington where spring would already be in evidence and a hint of summer would warm the air.

'You do look exhausted,' Megan said as she came in, carrying a tray of coffee and pastries.

Jessica turned to her. 'And you look positively glowing. What has the doctor put you on? Mega-vitamins?'

Megan put the tray down and beamed at Jessica. 'Keep it up. Now that I've lost my figure, I'm desperate for compliments.'

'Really, Meg, you look terrific.'

Megan was tall, blonde and still voluptuous despite the bulk of a nine month pregnancy and the formless blue shift that she was wearing. She had the slow, sensual grace that large women sometimes have and her blue eyes were round and sleepy looking. Jessica had always thought that Megan was one of the most attractive women that she knew. There was no particular beauty in her face; it was a bit too long for that and her nose was snub, but the combination of a creamy complexion, big blue eyes and a smile that was quick and warm was very appealing. Megan had the sort of face that made people like her on sight.

They had met as college freshmen and been friends ever since, spanning a ten-year period that included both their marriages, Jessica's divorce, living in separate cities and careers that had travelled in opposite directions. Megan was a free-lance sportswear designer; she worked less for the money than for the pleasure, having always been artistic and interested in clothes. It was Simon who was the main breadwinner in the Thompson family. Simon had been born to money, grew up with it and then made more. He ran a family firm that made parts for the automotive industry and had recently moved into aerospace.

Their apartment reflected his wealth in a quiet sort of way; its floors were carpeted with muted Oriental rugs, the furniture was leather and rosewood, and original paintings hung on the walls. Megan, who had been born into the middle class, grown up with it and never expected anything better, referred to the apartment as The Castle and frequently poked fun at Simon's assumptions and pretensions. Jessica had often thought that the one reason that the Thompson marriage worked so well was that Megan was such a comedienne and Simon such a great straight man.

Megan yawned luxuriously as she sat down opposite Jessica. 'It pays to be rich and pregnant. I haven't lifted a finger since the diagnosis and Simon pampers me to within an inch of my life.'

'I wouldn't complain.'

'I don't, I love the attention. And his mother is falling all over herself to be nice to me—sacred vessel that I am.'

'Sacred vessel?'

'*Dahling*—I'm carrying the Thompson heir to millions.'

'Maybe it will be a girl?'

'God, no. My mother-in-law believes in seances and Ouija boards and the dearly departed are predicting a ten-pounds bouncing baby boy with dark eyes like his father and blond hair like mine.'

Jessica smiled incredulously. 'I didn't know that Simon's mother believed in that sort of stuff!'

'Simon's family is rotten with eccentric types—it comes from having too much money.'

'But Simon seems quite . . . normal.'

'So far,' Meg said with a grin. 'He claims that his only peculiarity was marrying me.'

'Better you than what's-her-name—that red-head who was engaged to him first.'

Megan gave a dramatic shudder. 'She would have eaten him alive, poor man. Stealing him right out from under her nail-polished claws was one of the kindest things I've ever done.'

'You're all heart, Meg,' Jessica replied and they gave one another conspiratorial grins. Megan had taken one look at Simon, decided that she wanted him and gone after him with single-minded fervour. It hadn't mattered that he came from a different strata of society or that he was already engaged. The truth was that Simon had never exactly known what had hit him. As far as he saw it he kept crossing paths with a woman he had met who walked a dog in Central Park. He didn't learn that the dog wasn't Megan's until several months later, and by then he was hooked. His engagement was ended, its break-up supplying the gossip columns with several days' speculations, but Simon could not have cared less. He had fallen hard for Megan and was determined to marry her although she insisted that living together was sufficient. Not until she thought the moment was ripe, when Simon was particularly persuasive and his family frantic beyond measure, did Megan finally surrender. The entire operation, from baiting the hook to snaring the fish as she put it, took three months. The irony of it all, she told Jessica, was that she was madly in love with Simon and had been from the day her friend's dog had knocked him over in the park, put his filthy paws on Simon's cashmere sweater and been actually petted in return. 'Any man,' she said, 'who could put up with that had to be able to put up with me.'

Megan now leaned forward, poured them both a cup of coffee and handed Jessica a Danish pastry. 'Eat,' she commanded. 'You're too thin.' She took a large bite of a pastry herself and added, 'So how does it feel to be famous?'

'I'm just a nine day wonder. It should be over soon.'

'Oh, I don't know,' Megan said. 'You've touched a

nerve. Everyone I know is talking about *All's Fair*.
Either they hate it or love it.'

'Most of the interviewers hated it.'

'They were men, I bet.'

Jessica shook her head in despair. 'I just wrote what
people said, Megan. I didn't make anything up. It was a
big reporting job, that's all.'

Megan gave her a shrewd look. 'Don't you think it
was the tiniest bit biased against men? I mean
Simon . . .'

'You're very lucky,' Jessica said. 'Rarely is a marriage
as good as yours. Look at what's happened to those of us
who went to college together. Almost everyone's divorced
except you—Marci, Jane, Donna, me . . .'

'Speaking of which,' Megan interrupted, 'I heard
from Philip.'

Jessica went rigid. 'I don't think I want to . . .'

'He was in an accident, Jess. It was reported in the
paper, but the hospital played down how serious it
was.'

'I'm sorry to hear about it,' she said coldly.

Megan leaned forward, her blue eyes earnest. 'He'll
never drive again, Jess. It's the end of his dreams.'

'Meg, I'm not married to Philip any more. I'm
sorry that he's been hurt, but,' she held out her hands
in a beseeching sort of way, 'I don't want to get
involved with him again. It was too awful; I couldn't
bear it.'

They sat for a moment in silence as they both
remembered the traumatic years of Jessica's marriage.
Jessica, leaning forward to pick up her cup of coffee,
found that her hands were trembling and she clenched
them into fists. Even the mention of Philip's name was
enough to make her start shaking and she despised her
weakness. She had believed she was over him; the
divorce had been finalised three years ago and the
marriage had been sterile and empty long before that.
She no longer thought about Philip if she could help it;

she had pushed the memories into some dark corner of her mind, hoping that they would fade into oblivion. And both Simon and Megan had been kind enough before this not to talk about Philip, although Jessica knew that they were in touch. It had been Simon who had introduced her to Philip at that fateful party, bringing her to meet the man who had recently raced at Watkins Glen and won. He had been surrounded by women then, a glittering group of beautiful women, but when their eyes had met . . .

'Jess, I know it was hard, but Philip has changed.'

Jessica shook her head firmly. 'I don't ever want to see him again.'

Megan sat back and sighed. 'I just thought there might be a chance . . .' her voice trailed off.

'Not a chance,' Jessica said slowly. 'Not a chance in hell.'

The thought that there was even the remotest opportunity that her path and Philip's might ever cross caused Jessica to frown, giving her face a cold, aloof air that caused the people she passed in the plane to stare at her in curiosity and then look away. Jessica was tall, slender and beautiful in an austere but elegant way. She had not attracted male attention as an adolescent; she had been too gawky then, but during her early twenties the lines of her body had softened while her face had matured. Philip had been the first man to notice that her brown eyes were velvety dark beneath the uncompromising black line of her eyebrows and that the lower lip of her mouth had a sensual curve. Her face was oval, her nose straight, and there was a small cleft in her chin. Without being aware of it, Jessica had a regal look that could frighten off men when she combined it with her usual indifference.

The divorce from Philip had marked a turning point in her life both professionally and privately. She'd completed graduate school and found that her interests lay in exploring the relationships between men and women. She was honest enough with herself to concede that the subject held a certain fascination because of her own marriage, and she knew that she was still searching for the reasons behind its failure. At first, she had delved into the subject of battered wives, wryly acknowledging the bond that she had with women whose husbands beat them so brutally. Philip, it was true, had never laid a hand on her, but emotionally she'd been battered within an inch of her sanity. From there, she had gone on to study the rising divorce rate and developed a theory, admittedly controversial, about the willingness of men to remain committed to their women. Monogamy, she had written in *All's Fair*, was contrary to basic male behaviour. The brouhaha that the book aroused in critical circles was enormous, but Jessica had held to her guns throughout. She had talked to too many divorcees, too many unhappy women with stories of philandering husbands to believe that the majority of men were either faithful or loyal. And her own marriage was as telling as the others. Philip, she understood now, had wanted out from almost the beginning.

And the divorce had had its emotional toll, changing her personality until the Jessica of her early 20's was no more. She had been softer then, more naïve about the way the world worked, more eager to believe in such idealistic notions as love and caring and far, far more vulnerable to slights and hurts. When she looked back on herself at twenty, Jessica could now see why Philip had so easily led her down the rosy path of illusions. She'd been a sitting duck, falling for him immediately, dazzled by his dark good looks, his air of confidence and the fame that had just started to come his way as a world-class race driver. They had lived together for four years, a time marked by frequent separations because of Philip's profession and an increasing number of acrimonious fights and battles. The final one had caused Philip to leave, and it was then that Jessica began her metamorphosis. She grew cynical about men and tough about life. She threw herself into her work, having made the decision that marriage was not for her. And unlike her friends who were divorced, Jessica remained celibate. The sensuality that Philip had brought out in her had died, it seemed, along with her marriage.

But even if she no longer believed that she would ever marry again, Jessica deeply missed not having any children. She was happy for Megan who had tried for two years to get pregnant, but try as she might Jessica could not help her feelings of envy. She had an adoration for babies, for their tender toothless smiles and soft bald heads. The tininess of their hands and feet made a lump come to her throat and, lately, she had found herself daydreaming about having a child of her own. She could have tried to adopt; it wasn't unknown for single women to get children, but Jessica knew that her yearning for a child included the experience of having one. She had come so close once, if only . . .

'Taxi, miss?'

Jessica was taken out of her reverie to discover that she had automatically disembarked from the plane and walked out to the front of the terminal, carrying her suitcase in her hand. She shook her head in dazed wonder at her self-absorbed concentration as she now took in the hustle and bustle around her. National Airport was, as always, incredibly busy. Cars, buses and taxis fought either to get out or to find parking places. There was a constant rush of sound, of horns blaring and tyres squealing. Pedestrians crossed to the terminal, taking their life in their hands, while porters raced to grab their bags. Jessica shaded her eyes with one hand as she stared down the line of taxis, the long rays of the late afternoon sun casting distorted shadows on the pavement and turning the sky yellow.

'Hey, miss, do you want a taxi or not?'

'Sorry . . . yes, please.'

The taxi sped on to the parkway and then over the Memorial Bridge and into the District of Columbia, heading into the north-west area where Jessica lived. She owned a house that had belonged to her parents before they retired and moved farther south to Florida where they had a condominium. Jessica loved her house; it held twenty-odd years of memories for her, most of them happy ones. She had grown up on the street and played under its trees and bicycled on its pavement. Both her parents had worked; her father was a lawyer, her mother had taught school, but she had never felt alone even though she was a single child. The area had attracted young families to it, and during her childhood Jessica had never lacked for playmates. Now most of them had grown up and moved away, but many of their parents remained and Jessica knew everyone on her block.

The result was that Jessica never felt as if she was living in a big city and had never had any fears about living alone. The house wasn't large; it was a small brick building with a central entry flanked by bay windows with sheer white curtains, and the street was quiet and tree-shaded, the occasional car or truck rumbling under her windows. She ignored any news about Washington being a dangerous city and never thought about the possibility of break-ins or burglaries. Jessica felt quite safe and quite comfortable about her house, which was why she didn't even notice that its front door was slightly ajar until after she had paid the cab driver and walked up the front steps.

Jessica stopped in her tracks and stared at the door in confusion. She was sure that she hadn't left it open and her neighbours, the Malones, who generally watched the house while she was gone, were always careful to lock it after they had put in her mail and newspapers. The house was silent and nothing outside looked disturbed. Everything, in fact, appeared quite normal and peaceful except for the opened door. From where she was standing Jessica could just see through the screen door and past the brass knob of the inner door to her shadowed foyer with its stretch of white carpeting. She wondered who had walked in that way and glanced up at the second storey windows as if they could reveal the answer, but there was nothing to be seen in them except the pale reflection of leafless trees in their glass panes.

A sudden breeze caught a tendril of her hair, blowing it across her mouth and Jessica unconsciously shivered. There was a thin warmth to the sun's rays but it wasn't quite enough to dispel the March chill that still hovered in the air. She tucked the collar of her camel coat higher around her neck and looked up and down the street at the other houses. The neighbourhood hadn't changed. The Burberrys had taken the wooden covers off their bushes now that there was no chance of snow, and Mrs Stanford had obviously just gone shopping as her car was not in her garage but pulled up to the side door with its trunk open . . .

With sudden decision, Jessica turned back down the path and walked quickly across the street and two doors down to the Stanfords' house. She wasn't actually frightened and had even, for a second, contemplated walking into her house, the thought going through her mind that if burglars had come, they were obviously long gone. But then commonsense had prevailed as she realised that there was always the chance that someone was inside and she might be walking into real danger. A danger that could include guns or rape or worse.

Mrs Stanford was in her kitchen putting away groceries. She was the oldest person on the block, almost eighty and keen of eye, humour and vitality, a small woman with curly, white hair and now quite bent over with arthritis. She was widowed, lived by herself, still drove her car and was fiercely independent, never knowing that her neighbours' visits, friendly though they were, masked a real concern for her health and safety. She had fallen about two years ago and hurt one hip which she still favoured occasionally by walking with a cane.

'I saw you on television,' she informed Jessica as she energetically yanked open a cupboard. 'The interviewer gave you a hard time. Didn't much like you.'

'None of the men did,' Jessica said.

'Mmmm, can't say I blame them after the things you wrote.'

'The male ego is fragile.'

'You're pretty hard on it, Jess.'

Jessica smiled as Mrs Stanford rummaged through another bag and brought out a head of lettuce. The old lady had read everything Jessica had ever written and they frequently discussed it, often arguing in an amiable sort of way. Jessica put Mrs Stanford's disagreement with her theories down to the generation gap. Her marriage had lasted forty years—all happy ones, she insisted, although Jessica was sceptical. She knew how people, especially older ones, had a penchant for looking at the past through rose-coloured glasses.

'Did you see anyone go into my house?' she asked.

Mrs Stanford looked up at her quickly. 'You've been burglarized?'

'I don't know. The door was open and I didn't dare go in.'

Jessica followed Mrs Stanford to her front porch where the old lady stared at Jessica's house and pursed her lips together, shaking her head. 'Never saw a soul,' she said. 'Are any windows broken?'

'No, it looks quite peaceful.'

'I think you should phone the police.'

Jessica nodded slowly. 'That's what I was thinking.'

The police arrived in two white cars with black insignias on the side. They came quietly and quickly, pulling up before Mrs Stanford's house and knocking on her door. There were four of them; all tall, serious and very adamant that Jessica had done the wise thing by not entering her house at all. She and Mrs Stanford followed them down the street but were not allowed any closer to the house than the neighbour's hedge. They watched as the policemen cased the outside of the house and then very carefully, with their guns drawn, kicked the front door open even further and entered.

The wait seemed interminable and when Mrs Stanford shivered in her thin sweater, Jessica suggested that she go back home. 'I'll give you a call,' she promised. 'You'll get pneumonia standing out here.'

'I don't like the thought of burglars,' Mrs Stanford said, shaking her white curls vehemently.

'Maybe it's just some kids fooling around,' Jessica said soothingly. 'I'll let you know just as soon as I find out.'

She watched Mrs Stanford return to her house and then turned her attention back to her own. Although there wasn't a sound that she could hear, Jessica's vivid imagination was running at full speed. At first, she had been merely glad that she personally was safe, but now she began to worry about her possessions. Had vandals entered and broken her things? Jessica saw her living room in shreds, the oatmeal-coloured couch ripped and torn, her glass coffee table shattered. Or had there been burglars looking for silver and jewellery? She had no sterling but she had several strands of gold chains; pearls that belonged to her grandmother and a diamond watch that her parents had given to her. She was in the midst of a horrible vision of her bedroom destroyed: drawers of clothes dumped on the floor, curtains pulled to the ground, her fourposter bed pulled apart, when one of the policemen came out of the house and walked up to her.

'Miss Harley, will you please come with me?'

Jessica discovered that her mouth had suddenly gone so dry that she couldn't even speak. Wordlessly, she picked up her suitcase and walked beside the tall policeman, entering the house, almost closing her eyes in apprehension.

To her astonishment, the living and dining rooms were exactly as she had left them. The curtains had been drawn so each room was shuttered, the dim light touching on the dark wood of her dining table, the brass legs of her coffee table. Jessica glanced up at the policeman. 'No one has even touched . . .'

'This way.'

She followed him up the carpeted stairs, their feet making no sound as they mounted to the second floor. She found the three other policemen standing before her bedroom door and, turning to her as she approached, they beckoned her to look inside. Jessica clenched her teeth together, straightened her shoulders, took a deep breath and walked towards the threshold. To her utter astonishment, there was nothing odd or strange about the room at all. The shades were opened slightly so that a single ray of afternoon sun illuminated the deep gold of the carpet, the antiqued white of her dresser and creamy, patterned thickness of her bedspread. Nothing was out of place except for the bedcovers. They had been pulled down so that a man could sleep there, a man who was sleeping so heavily that he had not heard the police enter and was completely unaware of the audience that watched him as he turned slightly, his bare shoulder brown against the white of the sheets.

Jessica stared at him in horror and dismay. Not even the stubble of dark beard or the pallor of his skin could hide the man's good looks. His thick brown hair, longish and straight, lay tumbled on his broad forehead. The closed eyes were pale half-moons, the dark lashes were thin crescents against his high cheekbones. The mouth, half-remembered in her dreams, was softer in sleep, less incisive, less hurtful. Philip had always been beautiful in bed; she had often woken early to watch him sleep, knowing that it was unusual for his guard to be down. He had been hers completely then, for those brief moments before his eyes would open: silvery-grey, watchful and wary.

'He didn't break in,' one of the policemen said in an undertone. 'He had a key.'

Jessica nodded. Her family had always kept an extra key behind a loose brick on the dining room windowsill. They had done it as long as she remembered, and she'd kept up the practise herself. Anyone familiar with the Harleys knew where the extra key was.

Another one added, 'We can get him out of here for you.' He was smiling slightly as if he imagined a lover's quarrel, a small domestic matter. 'If you want us to, that is.'

Jessica was tempted to say yes. There was something very satisfying in the thought of those policemen dragging Philip out of her bed and house, but when she glanced back at the sleeping man, she was again caught by those rare, sweet memories. 'No,' she said, shaking her head reluctantly, 'you can leave him. It's . . . only my ex-husband.'

CHAPTER TWO

JESSICA expected Philip to wake up sometime during the evening, but she never heard a sound behind the closed door to his room. She thought it odd, but then shrugged and unpacked in the second bedroom, checked her mail and the messages on her answering machine and drove to the corner store to get some groceries for the next morning's breakfast. On her return, she took a shower and then went to bed, annoying herself by tip-toeing around the second floor and jumping at any noise in the house. She found the silence eerie and uncomfortable and she knew that Philip's presence, sleeping or not, was causing the tension inside her to build up to a highly-charged level, making her heart beat rapidly and her pulse race towards that inevitable moment when they would meet and she would have to face him again. It was a foregone conclusion that she hardly slept and awoke the next morning before the sun had risen and her room was still grey with dawn shadows.

It was ironic, Jessica thought as she flipped on the kitchen lights and began making coffee, that she would anticipate with so much trepidation and revulsion a man who had once taken her heart so completely. She had fallen in love with him immediately, his charm and magnetism enveloping her from the moment he had walked through the circle of admiring women, taken her hand in his and smiled down into her eyes. Philip had a way of making Jessica feel as if she was the only woman worth noticing in the room, as if she held some special glow that made her unique and valuable.

They had talked a bit; Jessica could no longer

remember what they had said, but the words had not been as important as the feeling generated between them. It pulled at her, causing her eyes to turn towards him, to seek a glimpse of his broad shoulders through the throng of guests. And often their glances had crossed as if he too felt that magnetic attraction. Jessica hadn't at all been surprised when he asked to drive her home and nor was she deceived by the polite way he said good-night to her. There was an undercurrent of desire even in that brief parting and she knew that she would see him again.

The courtship had been as heady as it was whirlwind; dinners, dancing, soft summer nights walking under the moon and the seductive appeal of kisses exchanged under the brilliant pinpoints of stars in the black sky. Philip had been free that summer to do as he pleased and Jessica had no classes. It had seemed as if they had all the time in the world to discover one another, and they did so with what Jessica now saw as an awe-inspiring leisure. There had been no hurry to the deepening of their embraces; Philip had set a pace that had caused Jessica no alarm and, when they finally did sleep together, the act seemed to be a logical and wonderful extension of their intimacy. Looking back, Jessica remembered the months before her marriage to Philip as an enchanted summer when reality had been suspended, when all the world smiled at them and when it seemed that nothing could break the closeness of those long, hot afternoons, their bodies so close and entwined that Jessica had heard Philip's heart beat as her own.

And he had been able to make her laugh the way no one else had ever been able to; she had loved his dry wit and devil-may-care gallantry. He had a charming ability to laugh in the face of fate and Jessica had, mistakenly she now thought, attributed this to an inexhaustible courage. But once she had separated from Philip, she came to believe that his cool bravery masked an underlying and deep vein of fear. During the brief span of their marriage, Philip had watched three racing friends die, their cars crashing and exploding into flames. She had not seen his grief; he hadn't permitted anyone to get that close, but Jessica was convinced that somewhere inside Philip had mourned and been afraid for himself despite the way he had brushed off her concern and her voiced fear that he too would die, locked into a burning car and consumed by fire.

She had wanted to know what made Philip tick, but she had never been successful. As their relationship deteriorated, Philip's wit had developed into a biting, hurting sarcasm and his flippancy had made Jessica want to scream. Disillusion had followed illusion as surely as night follows day, until she no longer recognised the man she had married or the emotions that had put the ring on her finger in the first place. She had tried, desperately tried, to be the kind of wife she thought that Philip wanted, but somehow it had not been enough and somewhere she had lost him, a moment in time that Jessica had never been able to identify. All she knew was that Philip no longer wanted or needed her.

Certainly his first race after their wedding had proven that. She had watched his car flip over with her heart in her throat and had seen his motionless body pulled from the wreck. The grey and brown decor of the hospital waiting room was forever etched into her memory, as was the face of the doctor who came to tell her that yes, Philip would be fine but no, he didn't want to see her and had, in fact, adamantly insisted that she not be allowed in his room. Nurses had turned her away even as she had begged to see him, their smiles knowing and full of pity. The first seed of antagonism had been sown then as Jessica, full of confusion and hurt pride, had gone back to their motel room to stare at the four walls and cry.

And then the antagonism had grown in profusion, branching into every part of their life, separating them into enemy camps and finally cracking the very foundation of their marriage until there was nothing left but ruins.

The kettle began is shrill whistle, steam issuing from its spout, and Jessica, pulled out of her thoughts, reached one hand out towards it when there was a sudden crash over her head and the faint sound of glass shattering against the floor. She froze for a brief second, hand in mid-air, and then began to run, making a mad dash up the stairs and arriving at the top step, her heart pounding, her breath coming short and furious.

It was silent on the second floor and, as her breathing slowly eased in tempo, Jessica glanced uncertainly at the closed door of the master bedroom where Philip had been sleeping. She didn't hear him stirring and she frowned in puzzlement, wondering how anyone could have slept through that noise and then reflecting on the peculiarity of Philip sleeping for so long to begin with. He had never been the kind of person who required much sleep, and Jessica remembered many evenings when she went to bed alone because she was tired and Philip was not. She had thought it odd yesterday that the presence of the policemen had not woken him, but had come to the conclusion that his trip to Washington had been difficult and tiring. He had, after all, just been discharged from the hospital.

Jessica made a quick tour of the study and the two other bedrooms and then stood hesitantly outside the master bedroom. The other rooms were as she had left them with nothing out of place, and the only conclusion she could come to was that the crash and broken glass must be behind that silent, closed door. She reached out and knocked faintly on a panel, pulling her hand away quickly and waiting. She dreaded seeing Philip; she'd had a very bad night sleeping in the room next to his and anticipating the moment when they'd come face-to-face. Snatches of dark and disturbing dreams had alternated with what seemed like hours of wakefulness when she stared into pitch blackness and worried about what she would say, how she would act and what she would wear.

When she'd risen that morning and dressed, Jessica had gone through her closet with great care, having learned from her many interviews that, while clothes don't necessarily make a woman, they can certainly function as a shield against the outer world. She'd dressed in a cranberry wool sweater that was stylishly loose and a pair of grey slacks, conservative and concealing. She had pulled her hair severely back from her face and wound its black length into a knot, her make-up skilfully applied to hide the shadows left from the night before. The overall impression was intended to prove that Jessica had not only slept as soundly as a baby, but was also basically indifferent to Philip's arrival in the first place.

Her cool exterior wasn't much help when Jessica realized that Philip wasn't going to answer her knock on the door. She was puzzled, then confused and finally angry, the emotions bringing a flush to her cheeks and making a determined glint appear in her wide brown eyes. She hated playing games, and it was quite obvious that Philip was up to something machiavellian. If she threw open the door, she'd probably find him sitting in bed and watching her with an amused, mocking glint in those light grey eyes. He would say something sarcastic and leave her feeling uncomfortable and gauche; that would be a vintage Philip Masters' move.

This time, Jessica knocked more loudly, rapping on the door with her knuckles and daring him to ignore it. This time she was answered by another, fainter crash and then a thud, and this so unnerved her that

Jessica threw the door open and stepped inside.

The master bedroom looked like a small hurricane had passed through. The bed covers were in a shambles, twisted and pulled apart so that, at one corner, the underlying mattress was visible. The small night table beside her bed had been turned over, its lamp lying on the floor, the bulb shattered into a thousand pieces whose shards glinted dully in the plush gold carpet. A bottle of pills had fallen beside the lamp and burst open, its contents strewn next to the broken glass, a spattering of white tablets.

Jessica turned her shocked eyes towards the open bathroom door and suddenly noticed the bare foot that was protruding beyond the sill. 'My god,' she whispered and, forgetting all thoughts about her dignity or the speech she had rehearsed for this fateful meeting, she raced into the bathroom.

Disaster had struck in there as well. A ceramic jar that held scented soaps had fallen beside the sink and caused the second crash she had heard. The thud had been Philip, who had obviously lost his balance and grabbed the shower curtain in a desperate attempt to stay upright, pulling it down on top of him as he fell.

Jessica hurriedly pulled the curtain away, finding Philip lying across the floor, one arm slung over the edge of the bath, the other supporting his head, his eyes closed although their lids trembled. He moaned slightly when the light fell on his face, and Jessica stared at him in shock, hardly believing what she saw and not knowing what she should do. He wore only a pair of pyjama bottoms, one leg rolled up to accomodate a heavy white cast on his right foot. When she reached down and touched his bare back, she found his skin cool to the touch but filmed with perspiration as if his effort to reach the bathroom had been exhausting, and his face was ashen as if he were in great pain beneath his stupor.

Jessica remembered the pills lying on the floor beside the bed and suddenly understood Philip's heavy, deep sleeep the day before. No wonder he hadn't woken when the policemen had been there or answered her knock at the door. He was drugged to the hilt, and she wondered if he had left the hospital too early, before the doctors had thought he was ready. That would be typical Philip—to ignore advice and to fight his weakness by trying to act as if nothing was wrong, as if he was still strong and healthy. She'd seen it happen before; he had ignored his concussion after his racing accident although she had known that he suffered from blinding headaches, and he had once raced despite a one hundred and two degree fever and the flu.

If he were conscious, Jessica knew that Philip would be humiliated beyond belief. He hated to reveal an infirmity and had never wanted her sympathy. She had never been able to understand his distaste for human contact at a time when most people craved it, and had finally attributed his aloofness to his damned pride and stubborn nature. Now, as he lay at her feet, the long muscular line of his back curved against the bath, his virility transformed into the helpless dependence of an infant, Jessica felt the irony of it all. When she had craved the right to take care of him, Philip had denied her, but when she no longer wanted him he had returned, needing every bit of reluctant sympathy that she could muster.

Jessica bent down on one knee and touched Philip's cheek, rough with growing beard. 'Philip? . . . Philip!' She knew that she alone couldn't bring him back to bed; unconscious, he was far too heavy for her to support or carry. Urgently she shook his shoulder. 'Wake up!'

His eyelids flickered and his lips moved. 'Fall?' he whispered.

'Yes, you fell but I think you're all right. Try to get up.'

He muttered something and tried to lift his head, only to put it down on his arm again, his eyes shutting again.

Jessica was beginning to feel frantic. 'Philip! Try to sit up. You can't stay here.'

A frown passed over his face. 'Home?' he asked.

Home! Jessica sighed and glanced down at him in frustration. Did he think that he had come home? Was he so drugged that he didn't know where he was? 'All right,' she said. 'It's home and you need to be in bed.' She took one of his arms and began to pull. 'Up, Philip! Come on, get up!'

Jessica concentrated on trying to get him upright, but he was a dead weight and she finally sat back on her heels in despair, wondering how she was going to get him back into bed when she happened to glance at his face and found that his eyes were on her. They were as silvery as she remembered, light in contrast to the dark line of his brows and the thick brown-black profusion of his hair. Their pupils were slightly enlarged and she could see that he was trying to focus. He blinked once or twice and then the faintest hint of a rakish grin passed over his face. 'Fancy,' he whispered, his words a bit blurred, 'meeting you here.'

'For god's sake!' Jessica exclaimed in sudden exasperation. 'This is no time to be funny.'

There was a short silence. 'Deadly serious,' he finally mumbled.

'So am I,' she countered. 'I'm deadly serious about getting you out of here and back into bed, but I can't do it without your help.'

It took him a while to get the word out. 'Efficient.'

'Very,' she said. 'Now I'm going to pull you up and you're going to co-operate.'

'Can't walk,' he muttered with a frown.

'Obviously.'

The struggle to get him out of the bathroom and back on to the bed took ten difficult minutes. He was

so dizzy when he sat upright that for a while he had
to sit with his head in his hands while Jessica
supported him. From there it was an effort to get him
on his feet, and there was a second when Jessica
thought that they'd both go down as he put some of
his weight on the foot with the cast and almost
passed out again. Like some odd-legged, lumbering
beast they made it awkwardly into the bedroom;
Philip's hand heavy on her shoulder, both of Jessica's
arms around Philip's waist as she supported him. The
distance from the bathroom door to the bed was only
a few yards but they covered it at a snail's pace, and
Jessica heaved a sigh of relief when they finally
reached the edge of the bed.

'We made it,' she said.

'Loved the final stretch,' he said, his mouth twisting
wryly. 'The turns were great.'

Jessica ignored his flippancy. 'Lay down,' she said,
noticing the beads of sweat on his upper lip and the
faint tremor of his body.

The ghostly grin returned. 'Best offer I've had in
weeks!' he joked, but he obediently stretched out on the
bed while Jessica tugged at the sheets and blankets
attempting to restore order, and lay there with his eyes
closed in obvious exhaustion.

'When did you get out of the hospital?' she asked.

'What's today?'

'Thursday.'

He didn't open his eyes, but he frowned and Jessica
could see how hard it was for him to think.
'Wednesday morning,' he finally admitted.

'Were you crazy?' she asked him, frowning in anger
as she began to walk gingerly through the shards of
glass to the fallen lamp. 'You should have gone
straight home.'

Philip shook his head drowsily. 'Had to come here.'

Jessica picked up the lamp and then straightened to
turn to him. 'Why?' she asked, but Philip didn't

answer and she saw that he had fallen back to sleep again.

With a sigh that mixed concern and perplexity, Jessica cleaned up the bathroom and bedroom and then went back downstairs with the bottle of pills in her hand. She called a local pharmacist, read him the name of the drug and got a list of its reactions. Philip, as she suspected, was on a heavy painkiller that tended to make him exceedingly drowsy and disorientated. The druggist suggested sparing use unless his pain was excessive and, after she had hung up, Jessica wondered how many of the pills Philip had taken. It wasn't like him to take medicine; as far as she knew he preferred to suffer in unmedicated silence, so her only conclusion was that he was in agony, and she wondered what the doctors had done to his foot to warrant so much pain.

By the time, Jessica finally sat down to have her breakfast, she was exhausted and let-down. She'd spent an enormous amount of her energy being apprehensive about meeting Philip again and, now that it was over and hardly what she had expected, she felt drained and confused about her feelings towards him. She had once loved him with a passionate intensity and then hated him with the same fervour. She hadn't realised at the time how easy such emotions were to deal with; she'd been whetted on their fine, hard edges, but now she saw that passion was easy to understand and far less complicated than her present mix of feelings.

There was compassion; she would have been inhumane if she didn't feel sorry for Philip, but she was surprised by the absence of any desire for revenge. After all she had gone through Jessica knew she would have been justified in finding a certain amount of glee in Philip's predicament, and she could recall, quite vividly, the fantasies she had had during the last year of their marriage when she would have sold her soul to the devil for a means of paying Philip back for the hurt he had inflicted on her. But if there were any remnants of that black anger left in her, Jessica knew that they had been obliterated by the morning's events. She had, quite unexpectedly, felt a welling of tenderness, like a flower that had suddenly bloomed in the dry, arid desert.

It was, she supposed unhappily as she forced herself to eat a piece of toast, somehow connected to an undeniable pull of physical attraction that not even a three years' hiatus had been able to diminish. When she had helped Philip back to bed, Jessica had felt her fingers tremble at their contact with his skin and the sleek hardness of his muscles. She had thought that her ability to feel sexual desire was gone forever, but two minutes in Philip's presence had proved her wrong. The physical connection between them had always been strong, and touching him again after long years of denial had brought back sensations Jessica had long suppressed. She had loved the feel of his body beneath her fingertips, a body that she had once known as well as her own.

Memories flooded Jessica in a rush so torrential that she put her head down in her arms and squeezed her eyes shut. Philip ... kissing her as they danced, their first kiss, the music pounding around their ears in a beat as primitive and urgent as their need. Philip ... carrying her into his bedroom; they were both laughing because he had almost dropped her and she had been forced to cling on to his neck like a small child. Philip ... lying on a bed nude, tanned and lean against the white sheets, his hand reaching for her, his light eyes soft with desire. There was no end to the images of love that Jessica could conjure up as if, all along, they had been just below the surface of her mind, as vivid as coloured pebbles when seen through clear water.

'Damn,' she said raising her head and clenching her teeth together. There was no point in wanting Philip, no gain in wishing for the impossible resurrection of the past. Their relationship had frayed on too many sharp points; his coldness and unwillingness to share his thoughts, her tendency to fly into rages. Jessica was well aware that she'd had a temper that was easily roused but not easily controlled. Quick to love, quick to passion and quick to temper, Philip had once said about her and he had been right then, but Jessica had long since learned to master her emotions. She had grown up a great deal since Philip had left her, and she had no intention of losing that newly-gained maturity, poise and cool simply because he had come back into her life.

Which brought Jessica around to a question that had bothered her since the policeman had escorted her up to her bedroom. Why had Philip come back? The marriage may have ended bitterly, but the divorce settlement was quite simple. They hadn't owned very many possessions despite Philip's high-income racing money, and there had been little to fight over. Jessica had never understood why Philip was so resistant to making a home, but he seemed to prefer a scantily furnished apartment that held no sense of belonging; blank walls and anonymous furniture. They had divided things up equally and, as nothing had much value, it was relatively painless. There was nothing that Jessica now owned that Philip could either want or covet.

It did not occur to her that he had come to Washington to hide and what better place to find camouflage than with his ex-wife. No snooping reporter would ever guess that Philip Masters, down on his luck and quite possibly crippled, had moved in with her. The news items that had accompanied their divorce had made it quite plain that their separation had been an acrimonious one. Jessica had never found out who had blabbed to the newspapers and given away secrets about her personal life that should never have been seen in print, but it had taken her months before she could read a newspaper again without a sickening feeling of fear that she would see her name coupled with

Philip's in some malicious and snide gossip column.

Jessica sighed, gathered up her breakfast dishes and set about cleaning up the kitchen. She supposed that it didn't really matter why Philip had come; she was intent on getting him to the point where he could walk and leave. She wanted her neatly packaged life back again; days of researching and writing, her round of literary friends, the slow pace of her neighbourhood. She wanted to savour her peace and quiet after the hectic publicity tour and to begin work on her next project—an investigative look at unwed mothers. And, above all, she wanted to regain the serenity of her solitary existence. She didn't want to feel any unnerving jolts of sexual awareness at the sight of a man's bare chest or that shivery warm sensation that had come over her when she had touched the dark, angling hair on Philip's abdomen. All Jessica wanted was to be left alone.

'He's staying with you!?' Daniel asked some three hours later, his wine glass held still in the air, a look of incredulity on his wide face.

'He's too sick to leave,' Jessica replied.

'He can't be that sick,' Daniel said with a touch of sarcasm, 'if he made it down to Washington.'

Jessica tried to sound reassuring. 'He'll be up on his feet in a few days and then . . .'

Daniel put the goblet down with a grim air. 'Jess, this is the guy who had you so beaten to the ground that when I first met you, you could hardly walk.'

'He doesn't have that power anymore,' she replied coolly.

'It's a test, isn't it?' Daniel asked with sudden perception. 'You're trying out your wings to see if you can fly free of him.'

'I am free of him,' she insisted.

Daniel leaned forward, the silver strands in his dark

hair gleaming in the light of the chandelier. 'Jess,' he pleaded, 'you're leaving yourself wide open to more hurt and more punishment. Publishing two books and making the bestseller list are great achievements but they're not necessarily protective armour. I've watched you when Masters is mentioned and it's obvious to me that even his name can upset you.'

Jessica stubbornly shook her head. 'Not any more.'

Daniel sat back with a look of frustration on his face although his eyes held an obvious appreciation of her coiled dark hair, the pure lines of her face and the classic style of her burgundy suit and the mauve and pink silk blouse. Daniel was in his forties, a widower for several years with a daughter in college, and a man of elegant taste and sophistication; his suits were hand-tailored, his greying hair always perfectly cut and combed. He had none of Philip's lithe and careless masculine grace, but his stocky figure was attractive, a refined and careful product of style and good grooming. Jessica enjoyed going out with him; Daniel knew every fine restaurant in Washington and he had a gourmet's palate for food and wine. The restaurant today, for example, was chosen for its glamorous atmosphere and impeccable service. It was a congratulatory lunch, Daniel had told her on the telephone. While she had been on tour he had sold the paperback rights for *All's Fair* for a large six-figure sum.

Jessica had met Daniel through a college professor of hers who thought that her master's thesis had the potential of being made into a book, and wanted to introduce her to one of the few literary agents in Washington. *Lost Souls* was sold within the year and it was Daniel who had set her on the path to researching material for *All's Fair*. He was a highly astute businessman; he had developed Jessica's reputation, talked the publishing house into backing her work with advertising money and found a publicist who taught Jessica how to handle herself in front of a camera.

Without him, Jessica knew that her career would have gone nowhere.

Daniel now switched tactics. 'Why do you think Masters has come back?' he asked.

Jessica toyed with her Caesar salad. 'I think he's trying to avoid the press. He doesn't want anyone to know how badly he was hurt.'

'He told you that?'

'Not exactly.' Philip hadn't told her anything. He'd been sleeping when she'd left for the restaurant and Jessica hadn't wanted to wake him. She'd left a tall glass of orange juice by the bed and a note saying when she'd be back. The druggist had told her that if Philip had taken the recommended dosage of drugs he'd been prescribed, he'd be suffering the after-effects for at least twenty-four hours.

'Couldn't he have gone somewhere else?' Daniel persisted. 'Doesn't he have any friends or family?'

'His parents were divorced when he was a child and they ignored him after that. He has an older sister who lives in Seattle but they never kept in touch. And as for friends,' Jessica gave a helpless sort of shrug, 'he's a loner; he always has been.'

Daniel stared at her for a second and then gave his head a quick, angry shake. 'I'm afraid that I don't think he has any innocent motives.'

'There's no need to worry,' Jessica said soothingly. 'I've told you; Philip means nothing to me and he hasn't for years.'

Daniel ignored her. 'He wants you,' he said grimly. 'That's why he's back.'

Jessica's eyes widened in shock. 'Oh, no,' she said, shaking her head and feeling the old pain come seeping back. 'No, Philip doesn't want *me* anymore.'

'A man can change his mind.'

Jessica looked away from Daniel's concerned expression and watched a tuxedo-clad waiter present a bottle of wine to a couple at another table. Philip wasn't the sort of man who changed his mind—ever. He'd made that perfectly clear to her many, many times. No, she couldn't visit him in the hospital. . . . No, he wouldn't give in to her frightened begging and drop out of a dangerous race with a car known for its difficult handling . . . and no, he didn't want children cluttering up his life. Daniel's suggestion that Philip was back for *her* was ludicrous, Jessica thought with a bitter irony. If he'd been there that day when Philip had walked out, he would have known just how absurd such an idea could be.

Jessica turned back to him with a smile. 'I'll have him out of the house in a week,' she said, 'and really, there's absolutely nothing to be worried about.'

Daniel reached across the table and took Jessica's hand in his broad one. 'Whatever happens, I'm here. You know that, don't you?'

Her dark eyes flew up to meet his earnest blue ones. 'Of course, Dan. You've been such a friend . . . so supportive . . . so . . .'

'I don't mean it that way.'

There was no mistaking his meaning. Masked though it was, it was a declaration of love and perhaps even a proposal of marriage. Jessica had known how Daniel felt about her, but she had deliberately avoided thinking about it and had always steered their conversations away from any intimate topic. She wasn't in love with him, but she couldn't bear the thought of telling him so.

'Dan, I . . .'

'Hush,' he said smiling, his hand squeezing hers gently, 'there's no need for any explanations or discussions. I just want you to know that I'm around if the going with Masters gets rough and I predict it will. From all you've told me about him, he lacks any compassion or sensitivity and you're a woman that requires both. Don't let him upset you, Jess. I don't want you hurt.'

'I won't get hurt,' she vowed. 'I don't care what Philip thinks.'

It was one of Jessica's more untruthful statements, a fact which was proven later that afternoon when Daniel took her home and walked her to the door. She was accustomed to kissing him on the cheek and exchanging an embrace, but she had seen the curtain in the living room flicker as they walked towards the front door and realised that Philip had woken and made it downstairs. She knew that his eyes were on them, and Jessica was uncomfortably aware of that gaze. It made her act awkwardly with Daniel; the kiss was perfunctory and the embrace was quick and hasty. She thought Daniel sensed her hesitation and knew the reason for it, but he was far too much the gentleman to make a remark about it.

Instead, he touched her lightly on the arm. 'Remember what I said.'

'I will.'

'And don't hesitate to phone if you need to.'

She swallowed, wondering if Philip had opened a window and was listening to them. 'I won't.'

'I'll call you tomorrow. We have more business to discuss.'

'Okay,' she said with a nervous smile.

'Jess . . .?'

'I'll be fine,' she said. 'Talk to you tomorrow.'

Daniel wasn't happy to leave her; Jessica could see that. There was an imperceptible shrug of his broad shoulders that was both frustrated and helpless as he turned away, and she couldn't help feeling sorry for him. She was genuinely fond of Daniel. Their minds met on the same intellectual plane and she trusted him implicitly with her business arrangements but, on her part, the relationship could go no further. Sometimes she wished that it could have; life with Daniel would be calm, comfortable and highly civilized.

Philip was in the living room as she had suspected, lying on the couch and dressed in a pair of dark slacks and a denim shirt. He still looked tired; there were dark shadows beneath his eyes, but he had managed to shave and comb his thick, dark hair into a semblance of order and it seemed evident that he was no longer under the influence of drugs. Jessica wondered how he had managed to get downstairs, but she knew Philip's iron will and determination. If it had been his wish to wait for her in the living room, such small obstacles as a flight of stairs and a crushed foot wouldn't have stopped him.

'Did you have a nice lunch?' he asked.

Jessica pulled off her dark sable coat and hung it in the foyer closet. 'It was very pleasant.'

'Who was your date?'

'My agent, Daniel Gilbert.'

Philip watched her sit down, his eyes taking in the slim cut of her suit, the elegant silk of her blouse and the triple strands of pearls around her neck. 'You look very successful, Jess.'

'Thank you,' she said and wondered how it made him feel to know that, while he had hit rock bottom in his career, she was soaring in hers. She never would have wished an injury on him, but she couldn't deny a sweet, inward satisfaction at the knowledge that Philip could see how she had triumphed despite all he had done to her. 'How are you feeling?' she added politely.

'The prognosis is survival.'

'Would you like some lunch? I bought some soup . . .'

'I don't want to talk about food right now.'

Jessica glanced at him warily, wondering if Daniel had been right about Philip's motives. 'What do you want to talk about?'

Philip leaned back, his arms crossed behind his head, the denim shirt stretched across the muscular width of his chest. 'The Washington Monument.'

'The Washington Monument!' she echoed.

'I'm going to climb it.'

'On your knees?' she asked sarcastically, thinking of the hundreds of spiralling steps in the needle-like building.

Philip waved a finger at her and grinned. 'A low blow, Jess. It's not worthy of you.'

She glanced pointedly at the cast on his foot. 'Do you believe in miracles?'

Suddenly, he was serious, the light eyes darkening with thought. 'Yes,' he said. 'I've become a believer in miracles.'

Jessica glanced at him in surprise. The conversation was not going in the direction she had anticipated, and this was definitely not the Philip she remembered. The Philip of earlier days believed in nothing more than hard work and self-sufficiency. Miracles didn't figure into his lexicon; he had been far too pragmatic, far too rational. If he couldn't see it, touch it or taste it, it didn't exist—like love, for instance, or caring.

'Since when?' she asked.

'Since the accident.'

Jessica raised an enquiring eyebrow.

'A hospital bed is a fine place for meditation. A man has nothing to do in it but reflect on his sins and,' Philip gave her a grin, 'wonder when the next bed-pan will arrive.'

Not quite a new Philip, Jessica reflected. He could still mock himself and anyone around him. 'And just what happens when a man reflects on his sins?' she asked.

'He comes to believe in miracles.'

She shrugged. 'I don't get it.'

The grey eyes watched her carefully, but his tone was light. 'As I lay there studying the past and then examining the future, a revelation came to me.'

The faintest sense of unease passed through her but Jessica ignored it. 'I've never known you to be religious,' she said in the same light vein.

'It wasn't a religious revelation. More of,' he paused, 'a marital one.'

Why did she suddenly have a sharp pain in the vicinity of her heart? Jessica knew quite well that Philip had had other women since the divorce. The same gossip columns that had so avidly reported the end of their marriage had eagerly followed Philip's post-marital affairs. Jessica had unwillingly learned about the rock singer, the New York model and the corporate executive. She'd known that he was the type of man who couldn't be without a woman, but she hadn't enjoyed having her nose rubbed into the fact. Still, she hadn't expected him to marry again; she had always assumed that he shared her distaste for the institution. For a fleeting second, she felt something very akin to envy for his new wife and then, aghast at the feeling, wondered why. Philip was no prize and *she* certainly didn't want him back again.

'You're getting married again?' she asked.

Philip nodded. 'I've wanted to for a while but the timing wasn't right.'

'Too many races, I suppose,' Jessica said casually, not aware of the way her hands were clenched together, her knuckles white with tension.

'You always thought I put my career before anything else, didn't you?'

Of course she had and, looking back on their life together, Jessica saw nothing to refute it. The racing came first and she had come last, playing second-fiddle to metal, leather and pavement, a bitter feeling for a woman who had been an only and much-loved child. Jessica pushed away the memories and avoided the confrontation Philip seemed to be aiming for. 'When is the wedding?' she asked.

'I don't know yet.'

'Isn't that a bit casual?'

Philip stretched, the muscles in his chest coming into

play beneath the thin denim fabric. 'Well, I haven't actually asked her yet.'

'But since you believe in miracles, you're convinced she'll say yes.'

He nodded. 'Something like that.'

'And who is the lucky lady?' Jessica asked with just the right touch of sarcasm to let him know that she'd never consider any woman he married as 'lucky'.

His eyes where shuttered for a second and then he turned them on her fully, silvery and mercurial. 'You, Jess. I want to marry you again.'

CHAPTER THREE

THE first thing Jessica did was to stare at Philip as if she had never seen him before. She noticed that he was thinner than he'd been during their marriage; there were slight hollows under the high cheekbones and his nose, thin and straight, was more prominent. There were also lines at the corner of his eyes that hadn't been there before, and she had a sudden quick image of a past moment when she'd seen him at the track, dressed in his bulky racing suit, his helmet in one hand, the other shadowing his eyes as he squinted into the sun, glancing down the curved length of pavement. Even then, his face and skin had had the texture of a man who spends a great deal of time outdoors. She had loved him so much then, before the bad times and the fights, when he'd seemed so masculine and mysterious with a core of toughness that she couldn't understand but only admire.

The second thing that Jessica did was laugh, albeit a bit shakily and without much conviction, but she laughed. 'You must be joking,' she said.

Philip gave her a grin. 'I've never been more serious in my life.'

'But we're divorced!'

'Damn,' he said, snapping his fingers, 'that's what my lawyer told me.'

Jessica couldn't see any humour in the situation. 'Philip, we were incompatible. Remember?'

'I'm not sure that I'd call it incompatibility. We were both too young. You were only 23 and I was 25. You didn't know how to be a wife and I sure as hell didn't know how to be a husband.'

It was an admission that surprised her but Jessica

45

wasn't convinced. 'You're right,' she said. 'It would take a miracle to get us back together again.'

'And you don't think it's possible.'

'I'm realistic,' she said, 'and to be frank, I hated you for years.'

Philip lifted a mocking eyebrow. 'There's always hope, they say, when a woman uses the past tense.'

Jessica lifted her chin. 'I'm indifferent to you,' she said.

'Are you, Jess?'

The question was spoken softly, but his gaze was direct and even and Jessica suddenly saw that, while she might have fooled Daniel, she wasn't quite capable of fooling Philip. She was no more indifferent to him than she could be to a storm that swept down her street, tearing the trees from their roots and shaking her house in its foundations. Philip's presence made her nervous, uncertain and confused. Her quiet living room with its soothing cream and gold decor was disturbed by the aura of masculinity that he projected, lying on the sofa, his shoulders broad against its softly textured fabric, his hair dark and thick on the gold pillow. She hadn't wanted to stay in New York after her divorce; the city was an anathema to her, and when her parents had suggested that she rent the house from them when they moved, Jessica had jumped at the chance. She had no longer wanted to live in a place that held any memories of Philip, and she highly resented the fact that he was here right now, upsetting the smooth serenity of her existence.

'Did you come to Washington just to ask me to marry you?' she asked coldly, standing up and smoothing down the burgundy wool of her skirt.

He looked up at her, his eyes slowly running along the slim line of her suit as if he were imagining what lay beneath the elegant cut of cloth, and Jessica hated the flush that rose to her cheeks, demonstrating all too clearly that she wasn't indifferent to him in the least.

He tossed the words out nonchalantly. 'That and to climb the Monument,' he said.

So that was it. She was merely another challenge, unconquered territory, an enticing treasure at the end of an elusive rainbow. The marriage had been a failure so Philip had to have another go at it to prove his invincibility. Nothing in him had basically changed despite Megan's statement to the contrary. There had always been a ruthless streak in Philip, a determination to get his own way no matter what the odds, and now that he could no longer race cars, there was no greater gamble than trying to win back an antagonistic ex-wife. Jessica wondered how long he had pondered his move while lying in his hospital bed. Had he deliberately calculated her sympathy and pity into his plan? Had he counted on the softness of her nature to bring her back into his arms?

Jessica felt a rush of anger inside her, echoes of earlier angers and frustrations spilling into the present like a river overflowing its banks, and all the tenderness and compassion she had felt towards him that morning drowned in its flood. 'You've wasted your time,' she said furiously. 'I'll never marry you.'

Philip smiled at her lazily, relaxed and easy. 'Why do I get the feeling that you don't think I'll make it to the top of the Monument either?' he asked.

'Because I don't,' she snapped. 'I'm afraid I don't believe in your miracles.'

The anger in her waxed and waned during the next week in an erratic pattern. It was difficult to remain furious with a sick man who, despite his bravado in being in the living room that first afternoon, was incapable of coming down the stairs for several days afterwards. And there was nothing false about his pain; not even a consummate actor could have faked the perspiration that broke out on his forehead or the white, taut skin around his mouth when Philip tried to put any weight on his foot. Meals had to be brought up to him; he often required her support to cover the short distance to the bathroom; and he was unable to endure long stretches of time without painkillers.

Over the course of that week Jessica finally managed to get a full explanation of his injuries. Philip had crashed against a ramp with such severity that his right foot, jammed against the accelerator, had come out of its boot as he had been thrown to one side. The foot, naked and vulnerable, had been caught between the edge of the door, a hot twist of metal, and the seat with its slowly burning plastic. He'd been pulled out of the wreck in time to save his life from the ultimate conflagration of the car, but it hadn't been quick enough to save his foot. There were crushed bones in both his heel and his ankle with extensive burning of skin. The surgeons had laboured over his foot and ankle for hours but the prognosis for recovery was grim. Philip would walk with a limp and he would never drive again; there would be no flexibility in his ankle at all.

When he told her that, Jessica had looked away, unable to bear the bleak look in his eyes. She knew how hard it was for Philip to think of himself as crippled in any way; he'd always kept himself in good shape and had had that casual grace of a man who has supreme confidence in his physical abilities. He seemed to bear the loss of his racing career with far more ease than she would have ever suspected, but the knowledge that he'd limp for the rest of his life obviously hit him hard. Despite his devil-may-care flippancy, Philip's feelings lay so raw on the surface of his soul that even Jessica hurt for him.

'No more dancing,' he said but his grin didn't quite come off and Jessica, her anger forgotten in sympathy, took his lean, muscular hand between hers.

'You never could fox trot very well anyway,' she said and he had, wordlessly, lifted one of her hands to his mouth and placed his lips against her palm. Jessica had pulled her hand away quickly as if it had been burnt, hating the sudden shiver that ran through her when his lips brushed her skin and the knowing glint she caught in the silvery-grey of his eyes.

They didn't talk about Philip's proposal of marriage or Jessica's reaction to it. When they were together they kept to non-controversial subjects; the weather, the news, Philip's arrangements with the doctors. He'd been referred to an orthopaedic surgeon at Georgetown Hospital who was going to put him through extensive physiotherapy. Philip slept a good deal, under the influence of drugs, and Jessica worked in her sunny, wood-panelled office trying to drum up some enthusiasm for unwed mothers. She arranged the relevant books and papers on her wide desk, sharpened her pencils, took the cellophane off a brand new notebook and sat there, staring at nothing more significant than the motes of dust that played in the air. For some reason the subject of unwed mothers held no interest for her, and she picked through her research material in a desultory fashion, her thoughts flickering in a thousand different directions; a thousand leaves tossed in a capricious wind.

Daniel caught her in that mood during one of his phone calls. 'How's it going?' he asked.

'It isn't,' Jessica confessed.

'Is Masters bothering you?' He asked that during every phone call and Jessica always gave him the same reassurances.

'He doesn't bother me at all, Dan, and when he begins his physiotherapy, he'll be spending most of his time in the hospital.'

'I thought you said he'd be out in a week.'

Jessica sighed at Daniel's belligerent tone. 'How can I throw him out? He's hurt and he's crippled.'

'And he's taking advantage of you. Since when have you become a nurse or a house maid? For god's sake, Jess, tell him to pack his bags and get out.'

'Perhaps when he's better . . .'

'Jess,' Daniel's voice switched into persuasion, 'you're being too soft. Be sensible; the man means nothing to you and he's taking up your time and your energy. Why are you putting up with it?'

A good question and one that Jessica had pondered frequently during the past week. There was nothing stopping her from telling Philip that he had to go, but she was reluctant to voice the words; something held her back. 'I . . . don't know,' she admitted. Daniel's heavy sigh came over the receiver loud and clear. 'All right,' he said, 'let's get back to the book. What point are you at?'

'No point. I can't seem to get into it.'

'Mmmm—I've been thinking, Jess, that you're going off track and that's the basic problem. Both your previous books arose from your own experience; you had a stake in writing them. This one isn't relevant.'

'But it's a good topic.'

'I have a proposition for you, and I want you to think about it clearly before you say anything.' He paused. 'What about a book on divorced men?'

Jessica's mouth dropped open. 'Are you kidding! I . . .'

Daniel murmured soothingly. 'Hold on for a second and listen. There's a number of good reasons for it. One: you've already written on the topic from the opposite perspective. Two: it would confound your critics and prove that you've got an open mind. Three: if you're going to insist on having Masters in the house, you've got one case study already before you.'

'Are you suggesting that I *interview* Philip?' Jessica asked in horror. 'That would hardly be objective reporting.'

'No, but it's one place to start, to gather information and get ideas. Food for thought—that sort of thing.'

Jessica was silent for a minute and then she said, 'You could sell this idea easily, couldn't you?'

'Jess, I think I could sell your grocery list, but I admit that a book by you about divorced men comes with some built-in attractions. I think we're talking about an advance in the million dollar category, to be specific.'

Her mind, fertile and active, was mulling over the idea. 'Money isn't the issue,' she said absently.

'But it doesn't hurt,' he reminded her. They'd discussed money before. Jessica, coming from a well-to-do background, never worried about finances; she always had the feeling that there was a net underneath that would catch her if she fell. Daniel, on the other hand, had come from poor parents and was a firm believer in a solid bank account. 'And don't think Masters wouldn't agree,' he added.

Jessica stared at the phone. 'What are you talking about?'

'Has it occurred to you, Jess, that he might be stone broke and that's why he's come back?'

It hadn't occurred to her at all; in fact, she'd always assumed that Philip had a lot of money. He'd won a number of lucrative races and got into the business of endorsing products like tires and motor oil. Even when they were married, the one subject they *didn't* fight over was finances. Jessica had never known precisely what he made, but there was always money in the checking account and she was free to spend it as she pleased.

Jessica had a hard time imagining Philip as a spendthrift. Unlike Daniel, he wasn't interested in sartorial splendour, fancy restaurants or fine wines. He preferred jeans and a shirt to a suit and tie, a hefty ham sandwich to a spinach quiche and he never drank. He didn't like to take anything that might impair his reflexes or his concentration. The only thing that Jessica could remember Philip spending money on was expensive equipment for racing, but even on those purchases he wasn't extravagant.

She sat for a long while at her desk, chewing over

Daniel's comments and finally rejecting one and accepting the other. She couldn't see Philip as a sponger, but she could see herself writing about divorced men if she thought about it hard enough. There was a challenge in it that appealed to her; she had enough of an open mind to consider the possibility that divorced men might have a story worth telling; and she could admit to an underlying curiosity about men in general. If Philip was an example of the species then she didn't understand them at all.

She piled her books and papers on unwed mothers deep in one corner of her study, gave them a smile of farewell and went out into the kitchen where she made up a tray for Philip. She was still smiling to herself when she pushed open the door of his bedroom, and he gave her a quizzical look as she entered and then glanced down at the bowl of chicken noodle soup she was placing before him.

'Did the chicken walk through this or fly over it?' he grumbled, running a spoon through the broth with its abundance of noodles and distinct lack of chicken. He was lying on top of the bed in jeans and a dark shirt, books strewn on one side, papers strewn on the other. Jessica could see columns of numbers on some and writing on others, as if he had been busy calculating and jotting down notes to himself.

'You must be healing,' she said lightly. 'You're getting grouchy.'

'You think you have me pegged, don't you?'

Jessica handed him a napkin. 'One used race-car driver with impossible ambitions, short on humour and long on self-pity,' she said cheerfully.

He gave her a sideways glance of his light eyes. 'So you're not angry anymore.'

'It's a ridiculous notion.'

He took a mouthful of soup. 'Why?'

She sat down on the rocker beside the bed and put her feet up on the mattress, wriggling her bare toes in the air. 'Because we both expect such different things from marriage that we're bound to be on a collision course.'

'Perhaps we've changed.'

'I don't believe that people change their basic personalities, do you?' she asked conversationally.

'No, but I think when their lives take a different direction, they discover that they may have different desires and needs than they had before.'

Jessica rocked slightly. 'You'll replace car racing with something else, Philip. And you'll be just as driven by it, if you don't mind the pun.'

His smile was cool. 'I was going to stop driving anyway,' he said.

'Were you?' Jessica was faintly surprised; racing had been Philip's only way of life.

'When winning loses its glamour and when all you see is the danger and none of the thrill, it's time to quit.'

'I never could see either the glamour or the thrill in it. The fact was,' and Jessica gave a small shudder, 'I hated it.'

'But you married me because of it.'

Jessica stiffened. 'I married you because . . .' she began and then came to a halt with a sudden reluctance to mention the word 'love'.

'You married me,' he said harshly, putting the bowl of soup on to the night table, 'because I wasn't one of your babyish boy friends who played safe little games in the back seats of cars.'

Jessica flushed. 'There's no point in talking about it,' she said.

'Why not?'

'What's the point of rehashing the past? Once you can walk again, you'll be leaving and . . .'

'I'm not leaving.'

She stared at him in consternation. 'You have to leave. You don't live here . . . it's my house and if I want you to . . .'

'We're going to get married again.'

Was he crazy? Had the pain and injury driven him mad? There was no sign of dementia; Philip looked very sane, lying across her bed, his dark hair ruffled on his forehead as if he had run his fingers through it earlier, his shoulders broad against the frilly lace edges of her pillowcases. Jessica knew that he hadn't taken any painkillers that day; he was far too coherent to be drugged.

'Philip . . .' she protested.

With one hand, he reached out and circled her bare ankle, his broad palm curving around her delicate bones. 'Jess, you're not looking on the positive side.'

She didn't pull her foot away; there was something very pleasant about the warmth of his fingers on her skin. 'A positive side to marriage?' she asked disbelievingly.

'Mmmm,' he said, sliding his hand so that his palm straddled the top of her foot and his fingers pressed against her arch, his thumb making small, casual circles against her instep. 'Two heads to solve problems.'

Jessica shifted restlessly, half wanting to pull her foot away from him, half desirous of the sensations rising from the sensitive skin on her sole. 'We weren't capable of solving problems when we were together.'

Philip ignored her, his hand rising once again to cup the ball of her foot, his fingers running up the centre of her arch with just enough pressure so that his touch wasn't ticklish. 'Two bank accounts.' His forefinger stroked the side of her big toe.

'I consider myself as independently wealthy,' she said, her voice just the slightest bit breathless.

His thumb ran smoothly between her toes. 'Two bodies.'

'Philip!'

But she couldn't pull away from him; he had a firm grip on her foot. 'Admit it, Jess, two bodies are better than one or have you forgotten?'

Jessica tried to look away from him and that narrowed silvery gaze, but she couldn't. 'I haven't forgotten.'

'Come to bed with me,' he said.

Jessica shook her head. 'No.'

'But you want to.'

'No.'

His hand tightened around her foot. 'Liar.'

Of course she was a liar, and it showed visibly in the sudden rigidity of her muscles and invisibly in the slow warmth that was invading the inner reaches of her body. Jessica wondered why she couldn't dredge up one iota of the anger she had felt towards him to stop the rising sexual tension within her. She tried to remember all the wrongs that had never been righted, the insults, the final painful blow, his arrogant proposal; but nothing came into her mind at all. It was empty except for a shimmering excitement and heightened awareness of the man lying opposite her. He was aroused; she could sense the stiffness below the zipper of his jeans and she had to forcibly quell an almost overwhelming urge to reach for him, to make him moan in wanting her. She'd had that power once and had exulted in it.

Jessica tightened her hands on the arms of the rocker. 'Sex won't change my mind,' she said.

Philip let go of her foot. 'But it would be good, wouldn't it?'

'What difference would that make?'

'We fit together,' he said simply. 'Not everyone does.'

They had fitted together superbly; sex had always been good between them. Jessica could remember long, lazy seductive hours in bed, Philip's hands and mouth caressing her with an intimate knowledge that had made her want and want and want. She had never been able to resist him and their fights, even the most bitter, had usually ended in a passionate love-making when he would take her with a breath-taking intensity. Shattering orgasms had left her limp and drained, disbelieving that she could ever feel that way again until the next time he touched her and the sensual miracle would begin all over again.

No, she hadn't forgotten their sexual compatibility but neither had Jessica forgotten all the rest. 'Unfortunately,' she said, her voice cool and slightly mocking, as she sat up straight, pulling her feet off the bed, 'there's more to marriage than sex.'

'Neither of us knew the first thing about marriage. My parents didn't set much of an example and neither did yours.'

'How can you say that?' Jessica asked in astonishment. 'My parents had a wonderful marriage.'

'Oh?' He gave her an enquiring look. 'And what's your criteria for a wonderful marriage?'

'They were compatible for one thing; they got along well together and they didn't fight.'

'It isn't healthy not to fight.'

'You think our relationship was healthy?' she asked in astonishment.

Philip pulled himself up against the pillows, winced slightly as his heavy cast shifted and sighed. 'Jess, your parents had one of the "deadest" marriages I've ever seen. It had no fire to it, no passion.'

She was outraged, incredulous and disbelieving. Of all the marriages that Jessica had witnessed, her parents' was by far the best. She looked back on the days of her childhood as a vista of sunny expanses and warm, cosy moments; the house running smoothly, every member of the family working in a spirit of harmony and co-operation. How could Philip dare to claim that her parents' marriage had been dead? It had been more alive than anything he had ever known; Jessica had been wrapped in a virtual cocoon of love.

'You're crazy,' she said angrily.

'They were friends,' he said. 'Nothing more. Your father was busy with his law practice and your mother immersed herself in teaching. They each went in their own direction; you were the only focal point in the family.'

'If it was so bad,' she said sarcastically, 'then why did they stay together?'

Philip shrugged his broad shoulders and wearily ran a hand over his eyes. 'Who knows why? They probably wanted to give you a secure home, and they came from an era when divorce was something of a scandal.'

Jessica, furious that Philip would try to impugn the happiness of her childhood, stood up and struck out at him. 'And now, I suppose you'll tell me that your family was a gem in disguise.'

He threw her an angry glance. 'My family was rotten and you know it.'

Jessica spoke with sudden venomous insight. 'You know something, Philip, you've always been jealous of me, haven't you? You couldn't stand the way my parents loved me and took care of me. That's what's behind this ridiculous attack on their marriage, isn't it?'

His voice was quiet. 'I was jealous,' he admitted.

Jessica was triumphant. 'Envy can colour your judgment.'

'I was jealous of the confidence you had that life would bring you everything you wanted,' he said as if he hadn't heard her. 'Your parents bred it in you; they gave you toys, books, bicycles, anything your little heart desired. I'll never forget your mother proudly showing me pictures of you in her album. Jessica on figure skates; Jessica on toe shoes; Jessica in the school play wearing a gown she had sewn; Jessica who had everything that love and money could buy for her. Yes,' and he looked up at her, his gaze direct, 'I was damn jealous for the boy I'd been, who'd never known anything but fighting and misery.'

Jessica clenched her hands together. 'I felt sorry for you,' she said in a low voice. 'Always sorry for the way you'd been treated.' She had, in the beginning, but eventually her pity had turned to frustration and then to anger. She could only blame Philip's parents so far in making him the cold, hard and reckless man that he was; the rest had been his own doing.

Philip frowned slightly, the dark thick brows pulling together into a straight line. 'But I wasn't jealous of one thing. I could see that all that love and generosity had its bad side.'

'Really?' she asked mockingly.

'I'm sorry to say this, Jess, but it turned you into a damned spoiled brat.'

Jessica was shaking when she slammed the bedroom door behind her, shaking with an impotent anger. She'd wanted to slap Philip, hit him, hurt him the way he had hurt her. Spoiled brat! *Spoiled brat!* What gave him the right to call her anything of the sort? Hadn't he always wanted everything to go his way? He had imposed his will on her to the point that Jessica had felt she was giving up everything that mattered to her. She had hated their bare apartment and the long, lonely nights when he was gone and the ultimate emptiness of their lives together. Was it being spoiled to ask for love and attention, to expect affection and caring, from one's huband?

Jessica turned at the top of the stairs as if to go back into the bedroom. She was spoiling for a fight with Philip, and she could feel the anger within her, tearing at her insides, trying to get out. She took a deep, shaky breath and willed herself to calm down, wondering why Philip was always able to set her temper off and then fan it into a conflagration. Noone else had ever been able to make Jessica so furious.

She stared at the bedroom door and made the decision in cold blood. Philip was going to have to leave even if it took calling back the four policemen to get him out. She wasn't going to put up with insults and smears on her character and that of her family. It was quite obvious now that Philip had come back for a number of reasons; his drive to succeed where he had failed before, the challenge of seducing a hostile ex-wife, a desire to rub her nose in her supposed flaws and, quite possibly Jessica acknowledged, to find a comfortable financial haven. For all she knew, Daniel's assessment of Philip might be more accurate than she had thought.

She started down the stairs and decided that she could have Philip out within a few days. His dependence on drugs was lessening, he was beginning to put some weight on his foot without pain and he was already starting to get around on the crutches he had brought with him. Jessica saw no reason why Philip couldn't go back to New York for his convalescence or rent a room near the Georgetown Hospital. After all, he'd managed to fly to Washington under far more physical duress, and she hadn't forgotten finding him downstairs after her lunch with Daniel. When he put his mind to it, Philip could accomplish small miracles.

The thought of the look that would be on Philip's face when he realised that she could no longer be conned and was perfectly serious about getting rid of him brought an inner glow of satisfaction, and Jessica walked into her study, pleased with the idea that she could get on with her own life and now fully determined to tackle a book on divorced men—the more she thought about it, the better she liked it. She had a feeling that all her beliefs and controversial theories about divorced men were going to be more than amply verified by research.

She sat down at her desk, grabbed a pencil and pulled her pad towards her when the phone rang.

Jessica picked up the receiver. 'Hallo?'

It was Megan on the other end, her voice filled with laughter. 'Guess what?'

'What?'

'The baby's coming.'

Jessica sat up in alarm. 'Right now?'

'Heavens, no. It's taking its sweet time; it must be lazy like me.'

'Where are you?'

'Sitting in the nursery, rocking in the rocker and watching the mobile over the crib swing back and forth. It has little wooden horses on it and . . .'

Jessica had a horrible thought. Megan was a bit eccentric but . . . 'Meg, are you drunk?'

'Of course not. I'm just enjoying the anticipation of it all.'

'Is Simon there?'

'No, and I haven't told him yet either. The man will go mad with hysteria, my mother-in-law will immediately bring out her tarot cards and . . . oops . . .'

Jessica gripped the phone when she heard Megan's ragged breathing. 'Are you okay?'

'Just practising the inhales and exhales. Did I tell you that Simon and I were doing childbirth classes together? He can breathe better than I can; the teacher gave him an A for the best panter in the class at the height of a labour pain. I almost died laughing.' She chuckled at the memory of it.

'Meg, be serious. How frequently are you having pains?'

'About one every ten minutes. Nothing to get excited about and they're not all that bad yet.'

'Promise me you'll phone Simon as soon as we hang up.'

'Ever the practical Jessica. Of course I'll call him, but I just wanted a few minutes to myself before the whirlwind hits.'

'Are you packed and ready to go?'

'Simon packed me a month ago. He's timed the trip to the hospital and alerted the doorman to hail a taxi the minute he sees our pale faces coming out of the elevator.'

Jessica laughed. 'Simon is very organised.'

'I always thank my lucky stars that someone in the

family is. If it were left to me, the baby would arrive into this world with nothing more to its name than a box of Pampers and a nightie. Simon, on the other hand, has been on a buying spree. The kid has ten stuffed animals, five varieties of teething rings and a diaper service ready to spring into action. . . . Oh, here it goes again. Hold on.'

Jessica couldn't help her death's grip on the receiver. Megan might have been nonchalant about being in labour, but Jessica was feeling every pain as her own.

The quickened breathing at the other end slowed down and Megan's voice came back on, strong and cheerful. 'Have you ever noticed, Jess, that Simon and I frequently have role reversal?'

Jessica refused to be diverted. 'Meg, I'm going to hang up and I want you to phone Simon right away. You're making me very nervous.'

'Not ready to do a delivery by phone, huh?' she teased.

'I left my forceps in the car. Now, come on, Meg. I mean it.'

'Okay, okay, but promise me one thing.'

'Anything if you'll get off the phone and stop being so chatty.'

'Promise me that you and Philip will be godparents.'

Jessica didn't answer for a second and Megan repeated her request adding, 'Simon wants you both, too.'

'You knew he was here,' Jessica said slowly.

'Now, Jess, don't be angry. There are rules about getting angry at pregnant women and . . .'

'You knew that I was going to come home and find him here,' Jessica persisted.

Megan's sigh was audible. 'All right, I did.'

'And you didn't tell me.'

'It would have ruined the surprise.'

'Megan! Do you have any idea how I felt? Do you have any idea what I'm going through?'

Megan's voice was hopeful. 'Philip's changed. Have you noticed?'

'I haven't noticed a damn thing,' Jessica said angrily. 'He's just as cold and arrogant as he ever was.'

'He isn't,' Megan protested. 'I saw him in the hospital and we had a long talk.'

'I'm kicking him out as soon as he can hobble.'

'Jess!' Megan was shocked. 'Jess, that doesn't sound like you. What has Philip said that would . . .?'

'He thinks he's going to marry me again!'

Megan was silent for a minute. 'And you've turned him down, I suppose.'

'Of course I have! We were mismatched in the first place; we didn't get along; we fought like cats and dogs. I hated him, don't you remember?'

Megan's voice was soft. 'There was always a chance that you'd changed, too.'

'Never!' Jessica declared hotly. 'And Philip hasn't either.'

'Why don't you give him a chance?' Megan suggested, her voice persuasive. 'Philip has his reasons for . . .'

'Don't I know it,' Jessica said bitterly. 'I'm strictly a challenge. An ex-wife who wouldn't touch him with a ten-foot pole.'

'Jess! You have it all wrong.'

'Come on, Meg. I wasn't born yesterday.'

'You're not being fair to him. He . . .'

'Fair to him!' Jessica was astounded. 'Is it fair for him to invite himself unannounced, decide that he's not leaving and hand out insults on my hospitality? I don't know why he thought he could come and . . .'

'He loves you.'

Jessica swallowed and stared out the window of her study where the low-lying and budding branch of a dogwood tree rose and fell with the spring breeze. A grey squirrel skittered up the trunk, paused for a second to give the immediate territory a quick scrutiny for enemies and then washed his small paws with hasty motions before running off again and disappearing from her view.

'What did you say?' she asked politely.

'He loves you, Jess. He always has.'

CHAPTER FOUR

MEGAN had a ten pound baby girl named Sarah Jessalyn that Simon, when he phoned the following morning, described proudly as a 'bruiser' with a shock of red curls. Megan, he told Jessica, had had a relatively short labour and uncomplicated delivery, and both mother and daughter were doing just fine. He sounded exhausted but elated, and Jessica couldn't help smiling at the boyish enthusiasm in his voice. You'd have thought that no woman had ever quite managed the feat of having a baby before. He made Jessica promise that she'd attend the baptism with Philip before he hung up and said that Megan would phone her as soon as she was up and about.

Jessica put the receiver down and lay back against the pillows, trying to imagine Megan as a mother and wondering whether her new status would change their relationship as friends. Before she had become pregnant, Megan had always been ready for a fling, like an impromptu picnic or a quick decision on one day to take a holiday on the next. Now, she would be tied down to an infant, and it really didn't matter that she had a maid and a nanny to help her with the mundane, everyday tasks like changing diapers and giving baths. A child was a responsibility, a sweet burden that harnessed its parents with invisible ties of love and, while Megan's sense of fun might not diminish, her spontaneity would undoubtedly suffer. Jessica recalled a time during Megan's pregnancy when the doctor had thought she might miscarry. She had spent a week flat on her back, chewing her nails and worrying at every odd pain and twinge. Megan had confessed then that she'd never really understood the grief that Jessica had felt after her miscarriage. 'I don't think anyone can, do you?' she had asked Jessica. 'Not until they're afraid of losing their own?'

'No,' Jessica had said, the memory vivid in her mind. 'No, I don't think they can.'

It had been, Jessica thought, one of the worst periods of her life. Her marriage had been disintegrating before her eyes and the pregnancy was totally unexpected, so much so that she had dragged herself to the doctor completely convinced that she was suffering from an incurable, unshakeable flu. The diagnosis of pregnancy had lit a sudden hope in her, a small flame of anticipation that the child could save her relationship with Philip and pull them back into some sort of harmonious whole. She had nursed that hope and let it grow, a small seedling that would burst into bloom at Philip's delight and approval. Jessica winced when she remembered how naïve and vulnerable she had been, carrying the child within her and believing that Philip would welcome the news of its existence with a new father's pride. She had, of course, let her imagination run riot with visions of pink and blue blankets, a small crib, a man's strong arms curved around a tiny morsel of humanity, so that the blow when it came was that much harder to bear as her dreams shattered around her like so many broken bits of glass, and her hopes withered and died, crumbling into dust and ash.

Jessica laced her hands tightly behind her head and, staring at the ceiling, squarely faced the memories; the twisting pain, the rush of blood, the medics forcing her to lie on a stretcher, the noisy ambulance ride to the hospital and the blessed oblivion of anaesthesia: blessed because it obliterated the knowledge that there would be no baby and blessed because she could forget that none of the faces hovering over her belonged to Philip, the man who had told Megan that he loved her, had *always* loved her.

Love. Jessica would have liked to know what it

meant; she no longer understood it herself although it was a word that she had once spoken with ease and conviction. She had thought then that she knew everything about love. It was all part and parcel of a high of excitement, an adrenalin-charged sensation that came upon her whenever Philip was near. She had been so positive then, so sure, that she had fallen into . . . love. What else could it be when her heart would race at the sound of his voice on the phone or at the sight of his dark head coming towards her in a crowd? *Love*. It was a word they had used with abandon as if it would flow out of the cornucopia of emotion forever. They had bantered it back and forth between them, teased one another with it—'Love you? How can I love a woman who grabs me the minute I get home, drags me into the bedroom, tears off my clothes and rapes me before I've had supper?'—and whispered it in the dark when their bodies were entwined.

Neither of them had been false; they had both believed it during that enchanted summer, but then something had gone wrong and the word disappeared into the darkness that had grown between them. One day Jessica noticed that Philip no longer said he loved her; on the next she realised that they no longer touched with affection. Sex took on a new aspect; the urgency remained but tenderness had vanished and they coupled mutely, satisfaction given and received in the cold exchange of barter.

Now, Philip believed that he wanted to marry her because he loved her, but Jessica was sure that he meant something far different; possession, perhaps, or acquisition. When she had needed his love and ached for it, he had withheld it, but now that she was free and no longer cared whether he loved her or not, he had come back to entrap her once again. Jessica saw that she had no choice but to make sure that Philip left as soon as he was able. She couldn't risk a repeat performance of her marriage; she'd barely survived the loss of Philip and the baby. The grieving process had taken a long time, longer than Megan had been able to understand at the time, but then she hadn't ever lost a baby or a husband or every dream that she had cherished close to her heart. And nothing, Jessica thought as she stared sightlessly at a long crack in the ceiling, dies harder than dreams. The baby, forever faceless, had become a nostalgic memory and she knew that she couldn't have lived with Philip, but she'd clung to her dreams with tenacity until a psychiatrist had shown her how her unfulfilled expectations of having the same life as her parents was feeding her depression to the point where she no longer cared whether she lived or died.

That was when Jessica had finally taken her life back into her own hands, moved to Washington and began writing the books that became bestsellers. Find a new goal, her doctor had told her, aim for different achievements. She'd found solace in her old neighbourhood and new worlds to conquer with Daniel. She didn't intend to relinquish her independence or give up all that she had accomplished for a man who had just come to the conclusion that he had always loved her. Philip had to go, and Jessica decided that she'd kick him out after Sarah Jessalyn's baptism. It was, after all, only three weeks away.

'So he's back, is he?'

Mrs Stanford had knocked on the door, brandishing a measuring cup in Jessica's face, and requested one egg and a cup of sugar. She'd then marched into the house and settled herself into the kitchen where she proceeded to engage in a bout of neighbourly curiosity.

'Yes,' Jessica answered, opening the refrigerator door and pulling out an egg.

'Been here about a week I'd say.'

Jessica repressed a smile as she reached for the bag of sugar. Mrs Stanford was well aware of when Philip had arrived, but she didn't know why he had returned—hence, her sudden interest in baking.

'What are you making, Mrs Stanford?' she asked innocently.

'What?—oh, some chocolate chip cookies.'

'For your bridge club?'

'Heavens no—those old biddies are always dieting. The last one served carrot sticks, if you can imagine. I am fully convinced that after everyone left, she pulled out a secret hoard of pound cake. Lizzy always was a fool,' she added, giving a contemptuous little snort, her white curls shaking.

'There's the sugar,' Jessica said, handing the measuring cup back to Mrs Stanford who set it down on the table and didn't budge an inch.

'Well, how does it feel to have an ex-husband in the house?'

Jessica had to admire her direct approach; Mrs Stanford obviously didn't believe in beating around the bush. 'He's really been sick,' she said.

'A good patient?'

'Not bad,' Jessica said. 'He can't get around very well.'

Mrs Stanford pursed her lips. 'I wouldn't think your Philip was the kind of man who could stand being crippled.'

Jessica ignored the possessive pronoun. 'He's taking it better than you'd think.'

'Mmmm,' one gnarled finger traced a pattern on the wooden table, 'bit of a shock, wasn't it, having him drop in on you out of the blue?'

'I was surprised,' Jessica admitted, pouring a cup of coffee and offering it to the older woman who shook her head firmly.

'Tea, thanks. Were you the only nurse he could find?'

'Philip's never been very close to his family.'

It was like a rapier battle, thrust and parry, Mrs Stanford's blue eyes shrewd and bright while Jessica remained close-mouthed and cautious. She liked Mrs Stanford but she knew how gossip could travel. The elderly woman would never talk to the media but she'd talk to her bridge cronies, the man who did her gardening and all of her relations. Someone would say something, the grapevine would quiver with the news that Philip Masters had moved back in with Jessica Harley and, in no time flat, she would find a reporter on her doorstep. Both she and Philip were newsworthy and Jessica knew it; she'd had to get an unlisted telephone number to avoid the constant phone calls she received from the press.

Mrs Stanford took another tack. 'Speaking of family, have you told your parents that Philip is back?'

Jessica shook her head as she added a tea bag to a cup of hot water. 'They're on a three-week tour of the Greek islands. They plan to stop in Washington on their way back.'

'Now, isn't that nice,' Mrs Stanford said, accepting the tea.

'I think they're making up for the years before Dad retired. He never would take vacations; he was always working.'

'Ben was a workaholic,' Mrs Stanford agreed, 'before his heart attack.'

Jessica froze for a second, standing before the sink, one hand holding a jug of milk poised over her coffee, her other hand clenched around the cup, the tension showing in her fingers. Then she carefully put the milk down and turned to face Mrs Stanford who was calmly sipping her hot tea. 'What heart attack?' she asked carefully.

Mrs Stanford looked up at her in surprise. 'Why, the one he had before he retired to Florida and you moved down here.'

Jessica stared beyond the old woman to a hanging that held a thick and luxuriant creeping vine. Her mother had made it years ago when she was in what she called her 'macramé and craft' phase. The house was dotted with such artifacts; a crewel work of an owl in the living room, a hand-embroidered cushion cover, a weaving that hung on the wall of the den. Dagmar had wanted to give her handiwork to a rummage sale when she moved to Florida, but Jessica had insisted that they stay. She liked her mother's work; each piece reminded her of her childhood.

'I never knew,' she said slowly. 'They never told me.'

Mrs Stanford shook her head and pursed her lips together. 'I always thought Dagmar was over-protective of you.'

Jessica frowned, not understanding why her parents had kept the heart attack a secret. Her father's retirement had come after her divorce from Philip and during the time that she was writing her master's thesis. It was true that she had jumped with alacrity at her mother's offer of the house and had never actually wondered why her father, who had so loved his legal practice, was giving it up to loll in the southern sun, but her lack of curiosity was no reason to keep her in the dark. She could have borne the news of Ben's illness, and it hurt to think that Dagmar had not only thought her not mature enough to handle it then, but had also never confided in her since. Jessica was almost thirty now, certainly old enough to know what was happening in her family and strong enough to be supportive. Her parents had aided her during the difficult years of her marriage. Why, then, hadn't they felt that they could turn to her for help?

Jessica sat down heavily in the chair opposite Mrs Stanford. 'How ... long was he in the hospital?' she asked.

Mrs Stanford patted her hand in sympathy. 'Only about a week. It was just a mild attack. My Herbert had one like that a good fifteen years before he died. It was just a warning signal to tell your father that he had to slow down a bit.'

'But he's only fifty-five,' Jessica protested.

'Ben drove himself hard, Jess. That's the way he was.'

They sat for a moment in silence while Jessica thought about her father; tall, silver-haired Ben Harley who had developed a large corporate practice and made enough money to give both his wife and daughter a very comfortable existence. There was the house in Washington, a beach cottage on the Chesapeake Bay, years of private school and university for Jessica and now an easy retirement in Florida punctuated by several vacations a year. There had never been any question that Ben could support their family, but her mother had always insisted on working, saying that she was bored as a suburban housewife. Jessica had accepted her reasons without question but now, for the first time, it occurred to her that perhaps Dagmar had worked because Ben Harley had been too busy to keep her company.

Jessica mentally gave herself a shake, furious that she had allowed Philip's insinuations about her parents to get the better of her. While it was true that Ben had worked long hours, Jessica could remember weekends of family outings; picnics, bike rides, skiing trips, and her father had always been there when she needed him—always.

'I wish,' she sighed, 'that they had told me.'

'Dagmar didn't want to worry you.'

'I'm not ten anymore.'

'A child is always a child in its mother's eyes,' Mrs Stanford said with a wise bobbing of her head.

Jessica suddenly leaned forward. 'Do you think,' she asked, 'that my parents spoiled me?'

The old woman's blue, hooded eyes surveyed Jessica's intent face and then she took a sip of her tea. 'In my opinion, most children are spoiled today. Take my grandson, Dennis. Frankly, he could use a good spanking now and then to keep him in line. If I've told my daughter once, I've told her . . .'

'Do you think they spoiled me?' Jessica insisted.

Mrs Stanford put down her cup. 'Now, Jess, you

were a very sweet little girl, but Dagmar and Ben did dote on you and it's only natural that you thought the world revolved around you. They couldn't help loving you and giving you everything you wanted.'

'Was I . . . obnoxious?'

The white curls shook emphatically and the old lady stood up. 'I'm not going to sit here and listen to you talk about yourself like that, Jess. You've been a fine neighbour and I've always enjoyed your company. It isn't worth raking through the past and upsetting yourself. Think about the future instead.'

'But . . .'

Mrs Stanford balanced the egg in one wrinkled hand while she slapped the other on the table to make her point. 'It doesn't pay to be too introspective, child. Enjoy life and take every day as it comes. You've only got one go-around, you know. That's what I always say.'

Jessica sat at the kitchen table long after Mrs Stanford had gone, her chin in her hand, her dark eyes unhappy and thoughtful. She had never realised the lengths that her parents would go to to protect her, and it hurt a lot that they hadn't trusted her maturity enough to confide their fears and worries in her. Had she always been so coddled? Had Dagmar and Ben been as over-protective as Mrs Stanford had suggested? She couldn't help wondering what other problems her parents had hidden from her. Other medical problems? Financial worries? Marital arguments? Jessica didn't like to think that her childhood had been a lie, or that Philip may have been right about her parents' marriage. It made her feel as if the ground was shifting beneath her, the very solid foundation of her life moving and cracking in disturbing, unforeseen patterns.

Jessica had a sudden and intent desire to go back two weeks, to be facing that interviewer once again with nothing more to worry about than her public image. Everything had been so calm and peaceful in her private life. The books were selling well; her parents seemed healthy; she had no money problems and the future only beckoned with further successes. Now, it had all been reversed and twisted. Her father's health was only ephemeral; she was no longer certain if she could write another book; and Philip's re-entry into her life had brought nothing but pain and uncertainty. Like a stone hurled into still waters, his coming had sent reverberations of shock into every corner of her life.

Cabin fever, not surprisingly, struck Philip as soon as he was able to get around on crutches. He made his first descent, slow but steady, to the main level of the house on the afternoon of Mrs Stanford's visit and announced that he wanted to go out for a ride, anywhere—he didn't give a damn—as long as it was *out*. So Jessica hastily pulled a jacket over her dark turtle-neck and cords and drove him down to the Tidal Basin where they passed rows of cherry trees, heavy with blossoms, their petals a thick, dusty-pink. The wind had picked up and the water was rising in white caps, the boats shifting restlessly in their moorings. It was one of those days that showed downtown Washington off to its best, the monuments gleaming white in the sun, spring so heavy in the air that the joggers were already out, running along the pavement, passing groups of tourists weighed down with cameras and paraphernalia.

Philip had rolled down his window and was singing into the wind, some song about going to sea and riding a storm. He had a pleasant deep baritone, and every once in a while Jessica would glance at him in reluctant admiration. He looked so relaxed and carefree, his dark hair blowing around his forehead, his hands tucked into the pockets of his denim jacket. No one would have guessed how fatigued he had become just walking out to the car and struggling to get inside without putting any extra weight on his foot. She'd seen his mouth twist in sudden pain and seen his knuckles turn white on the door handle, but he hadn't said a thing and once she had started driving, he'd begun to hum, breaking into full song once she was out on the highway.

Jessica couldn't understand how he kept up his spirits after days of enforced rest and immobility, knowing that if she were Philip, she would be hard put to smile let alone sing. But that was his way, she reminded herself with a touch of bitterness as she negotiated a turn through a crowded intersection. Never show a speck of emotion, bury any unhappiness deep within and display a brave front on the outside. It was the Philip Masters' creed and, as far as Jessica knew, he'd never let his façade slip or lost his composure in front of anyone, let alone his wife. She still wondered what lay below the superficial mask that Philip showed to the public. Every once in a while she'd catch a glimpse of another man, a man who could feel and hurt and cry, but such moments were few and far between. He always held the mask so firmly in place, the smile ever-ready, the silvery eyes dancing in self-mockery.

Jessica drove into Capitol Hill where the government offices were located and the sidewalks swarmed with lawyers, lobbyists and legislators. Philip insisted on stopping for a coffee and she was lucky enough to find a parking space before a well known restaurant that was famed for its stained glass windows and extravagant English pub decor. Philip managed to get out of the car with somewhat less difficulty than he had getting in, and Jessica breathed a sigh of relief when he skilfully negotiated the two steps to the entrance of the restaurant despite the awkwardness of having only one good foot and a pair of crutches.

They sat in a wood panelled booth with red leather banquettes and their coffee was served in deep mugs with monograms on the side that looked vaguely royal. The bar area was already crowded three-deep although it was early afternoon and the sounds of piped-in madrigal music was faint over the noise of conversation and glasses clinking. Philip leaned his head against the partition and was just about to speak when a woman came to stand before the table, her eyes wide in astonishment.

'Philip Masters! I don't believe it! What *are* you doing in Washington? Haven't you just come out of the hospital?'

They both turned and Jessica felt a sudden dismay, a sinking feeling in the pit of her stomach and a curl of dislike. She hadn't taken to Nora Speers when they'd first met, and long acquaintance hadn't changed her basic feelings. Nora was the type of woman who hung around the race tracks, eager to see and be seen, getting a high out of thrills and danger. She knew everyone; the mechanics, the managers, the judges, the representatives of the car companies and the drivers, especially the drivers.

'And Jess! Are you two an item again or am I being nosy?' She slid into the banquette beside Philip and gave Jessica an artless smile. Nora was neither particularly pretty nor particularly glamorous but she exuded something, a faint whiff of sexuality, a come-hither look in her big brown eyes that attracted men. She was petite, a bit on the plump side and very vivacious. Her greatest attraction was her hair; a thick honey-brown fall that framed her round face in waves.

'You're being nosy,' Philip said giving her a lazy grin.

Nora ignored the insult and gave him a playful pat on his hand. 'I heard you were immobilised after your accident and yet here you are—larger than life.'

'You can't keep a good man down,' Philip said idly.

Nora gave him a flirtatious look. 'So they say,' and then added persistently, 'Seriously, I didn't know you two were back together.'

'We're n . . .,' Jessica began when she felt a pressure on her foot and realised that Philip was warning her to stop.

'What are *you* doing in Washington?' he interjected smoothly.

Nora glanced quickly from Philip's expression of bland curiosity to Jessica's pasted-on smile. 'I'm on Senator Brockhower's staff,' she said in an absent tone.

'I didn't know you were political,' Philip drawled.

'I got tired of doing PR work on Madison Avenue and my family had connections.' She shrugged her plump shoulders and then put out a beseeching hand, her fingernails long and cherry-red to match the colour of her suit. 'Come on, you guys, tell all. I'm simply avid with curiosity. I thought your divorce was on the . . . unfriendly side.'

Jessica felt the pressure again. 'No, we're friends,' she said.

Nora burbled on. 'And Jess is such a success now. I've just devoured your books from cover to cover. They were *sooo* fascinating. Didn't you think so, Philip?'

'Yes,' he said slowly, 'I did.' And Jessica gave him a quick glance of surprise. Philip hadn't mentioned her books and she had assumed that he hadn't read them at all.

'Everyone is talking about *All's Fair*,' Nora went on. 'You've stirred up a hornets' nest. The men in my office hate it.'

'Men don't like to hear the truth,' Jessica said, uncomfortably aware of Philip's silver gaze on her face.

'Of course not,' Nora gushed. 'I've been divorced twice and you had my husbands pegged, absolutely pegged. The first one was a bastard from the word go. He didn't want to give up his extra-curricular activities—they were all female. And the other one was . . . well, perhaps boring would be the best word.'

Philip turned to her. 'And you left him?'

Nora opened her hands in a helpless gesture. 'We had nothing to say to one another.'

'The men in Jess's book left their wives,' he went on. 'You damned us all for that, didn't you?'

Jessica sat back, surprised at the sudden attack. 'Statistics show . . .' she began.

The smile he gave her was mirthless. 'Statistics prove nothing,' he said. 'Some men are driven to leave their wives.'

Nora's eyelashes positively fluttered in excitement as she took in the sudden tension at the table, and Jessica discovered that she hated her, hated the way she flirted with Philip, hated the way she hung on every word they were saying, a gossipmonger who thrived on other people's private affairs.

'Most women who are left are helpless,' Jessica replied, trying to maintain an air of rationality while she suppressed a desire to slap Nora across the face. 'It was their case that I was arguing.'

'Some women are too dependent,' Philip retorted. 'They're incapable of standing on their own.'

Jessica forgot Nora's rapacious curiosity. 'In this society most women can't earn enough money to stand on their own and support their children,' she fired angrily.

'I'm not talking about finances,' Philip returned. 'I'll grant you that women are underpaid in our society. I'm talking about emotional dependence, about women who are still children and cling to their husbands as if they were fathers.'

He had slid the knife in so easily and with such consummate skill that its pain took Jessica's breath away. The accusation had hurt then and it hurt now, couched though it was in abstract terms and spoken in an intellectual way as if the three of them were idly discussing a question of philosophy. But that final, bitter argument had been hardly philosophic; it had been intensely personal and highly vindictive. Philip had hurled names at her, calling her a baby who was looking for another father, a whining, clinging child who was suffocating him with her needs and wants. *Grow up*, he had grated, flinging the words at her so she had felt as if he had slapped her, the sharp sting turning her cheeks red and causing tears to spring into her eyes.

It took all of Jessica's poise to hide how she felt, to act as if Philip's words were nothing more than mere conversation. Her cheeks were flaming and there was a tilt to her head as if she had taken a blow on the chin, but she turned to Nora with a smile. 'Have you given up following the races?' she asked.

Nora's eyebrows made an expressive arch, but she was willing to follow Jessica's lead. 'I have a new hobby now,' she said lightly. 'I'm collecting politicians—they live longer, I've found.' Her very mobile mouth turned down at the corners, and Jessica recalled a rumour that Nora had been having a passionate affair with Fraser Damont, a race-car driver who had been killed at Indianapolis several years earlier. 'And what about you, Philip, are you giving up racing?'

'The doctors say it's advisable.'

'And what do you plan to do now?'

Philip shrugged his broad shoulders. 'I haven't decided.'

'You can probably live on your residuals. Didn't you make millions pushing gas and oil on television?'

'Perhaps I should go into acting.'

Nora clapped her hands in delight. 'Marvellous!' she exclaimed. 'What do you think, Jess. He has the face for it, don't you think?'

'I . . .'

'Turn your head, darling, so I can see your profile.' Philip obligingly turned so that he presented his profile to Nora and faced Jessica directly, their eyes meeting. 'Do you mind if I get rhapsodic about it?' Nora went on. 'I can already see you in something dramatic. You have that strong, macho look around the mouth and nose, and . . .'

Their eyes were locked; Philip's knowing, Jessica's angry. She didn't want to delve into the past, she didn't want to be dragged onto old battlegrounds. The wounds Philip had inflicted had healed very slowly and with great pain. Jessica had learned a lot about herself in the process, and not all of it was pleasant. She had acknowledged long ago that there had been some truth in Philip's accusations: she had clung to him, she had looked to him for emotional support and perhaps her demands had been excessive, but she'd been young then, too immature to understand that no one can be responsible for another's happiness. And Philip hadn't been blameless either. He gave only sexually; every other emotion was held back, locked away and marked 'hands off.' Jessica had learned early on that there was no probing Philip's psyche; he wouldn't tolerate any questioning, any sympathy or any desire on her part to get closer except in a physical sense. The only time that Philip allowed himself to be vulnerable was when they made love; only then was Jessica powerful, when he was naked, his pleasure found in her hands, her mouth and her body.

'. . . thrillers,' Nora was saying with enthusiasm. 'You'd be great as the detective hero, handsome and slightly mysterious.'

'I had no idea you were such a romantic,' Philip said.

Nora batted her eyelashes at him. 'All women are romantic. Don't you agree, Jess?'

'No,' Jess answered, 'I'm not.'

Nora gave her a wide brown-eyed stare. 'I don't believe it. Why, you used to just swoon over Philip. You thought the sun shone out of his eyes.'

Jessica avoided Philip's glance. 'I've changed,' she said. 'I don't think any man is the centre of the universe any more.'

'I don't believe any woman can change that much,' Nora denied dramatically. 'We all want roses and moonlight, intimate tête-à-têtes over champagne, and scads of diamonds and furs.'

'Are you sure you aren't talking about money instead of romance?' Philip asked drily.

'*Dahling*,' she drawled, 'you have positively no imagination and, frankly, I could never feel romantic over pork and beans. Money simply enhances the scene, gives lustre to sex appeal and adds a glow to the candlelight. Now, for example,' she added slyly, 'if you're trying to get Jessica back, then this place is all wrong for your first manoeuvre.'

Philip played along with her. 'Really? You think so?'

'A proposal requires a certain atmosphere.' Nora waved cherry-tipped fingers at the assemblage before the bar. 'Too crowded, the lighting is a bit heavy and who needs madrigals?'

'Too sedate?' Philip asked.

Nora gave them a frankly inquisitive look. 'Really, you two don't fool me in the least. I remember a certain night after Jess's miscarriage when Philip got drunk and poured out his heart over several double whiskeys. Admit it, you were both miserable.'

Jessica was slipping out of the booth, almost upsetting her mug of coffee which had gone stone-cold and unpalatable during Nora's visit. 'I think we have to leave,' she said to Philip. 'I have an appointment.'

Nora was too smart not to catch the hint. 'It's been great seeing you both again,' she said, wiggling out of the booth. 'Give me a buzz sometime and we can get together.'

She disappeared into the crowd and Jessica was silent as Philip put down some money to pay for their coffee and, grabbing his crutches, pulled himself upright. She didn't talk until they had pulled on their coats, walked out of the restaurant, seated themselves in the car and she had turned on the ignition, letting the car idle at the curb.

'So that's how it happened,' she said, staring unseeing out of the window, her hands gripping the steering wheel, her teeth clenched together.

'How what happened?'

'That's how the newspapers found out about the baby.'

He shrugged. 'I was drunk,' he said. 'Drowning my sorrows in the appropriate fashion.'

Jessica threw him a stormy glance, wondering angrily why he had chosen to talk about his private life to a vicious little gossip like Nora Speers. In all their married life, he had never 'poured out his heart' to her, and she had begged him, virtually on her knees, to please, *please* explain why he was so cold, so harsh, so withdrawn and so hurtfully cold.

'I didn't know that you gave a damn in the first place,' she said bitterly.

Philip's voice held a lingering pain. 'It was my child, too.'

Jessica turned to face him, her brown eyes almost black in fury. 'Then why weren't you there?' she hissed. 'Why didn't you come to the hospital?'

'Sweet Jess,' he mocked her. 'Have you lost your memory?'

She gaped at him. 'My memory?'

'You didn't want me. The doctor told me that you absolutely refused to see me.'

CHAPTER FIVE

THE news that Philip and Jessica were co-habiting (they'd never know how Nora found that out), and that wedding bells might be ringing in the not-so-distant future, made it into one rather sedate Washington paper and a New York journalistic rag. Megan clipped the article and sent it to Jessica with a note that she was only getting four hours of sleep at a stretch, had never really understood what a dirty diaper meant and would call as soon as Sarah Jessalyn, slightly colicky but otherwise absolutely adorable, gave her five minutes of peace.

The Washington paper had the item in their *'People'* section, and merely reported that Philip Masters, race-car driver, had moved in with his ex-wife, best-selling author Jessica Harley, while recuperating from surgery for injuries to his foot sustained during a recent driving accident. A second marriage was not actually mentioned, but the reader was given the chance to put two and two together and come up with four.

The New York paper, on the other hand, went in for sensationalism and blared the news in a large headline, *Divorce Can't Separate Lovers*. The article went on to itemise in excruciating detail the events leading up to Jessica and Philip's divorce, made snide remarks about the way Jessica's marital failure had inspired her writing and gave an in-depth and nauseating rehash of Philip's accident. The article was accompanied by two photos, one of Jessica emerging from the courtroom after the divorce, her face shaded by a wide-brimmed hat, and another of Philip's car burning up on the racetrack.

Jessica read both articles with a stony-faced detachment, but Daniel was far less stoic about them.

'This,' he said, pointing to the article with distaste, 'is going to hurt your image.'

She gave a helpless shrug. 'It was an accident. Philip and I met someone who knew us before and . . .'

'And he had a few contacts.'

'She,' Jessica corrected him glumly. 'It was a woman.'

'One of Philip's rejects?' Daniel asked harshly.

Jessica glanced up from her laced fingers in surprise. 'No . . . I don't think so.'

Daniel ran his fingers through his impeccably combed hair. 'Well, she sure as hell had it in for you.'

Jessica slumped back in her chair, an unconsciously graceful figure in grey slacks and soft grey sweater, and stared out the window of Daniel's office. He had a lovely eighth-storey view of the Mall, its yards of trimmed grass forming a long geometrically precise green carpet between the Monument and the Capitol Building. From a distance, people appeared as dark specks on the grass as they made their way to the museums that lined the Mall or merely strolled in the warm afternoon sun, and the Reflecting Pool in front of the Capitol glittered in iridescent flashes as if diamond chips had been sewn on to its blue surface.

Jessica had dropped Philip at Georgetown Hospital and then driven to Daniel's office, wanting to tell him in person rather than on the phone, that she couldn't seem to get started on a book about divorced men. He had met her quite graciously at the door, invited her to sit down on the big leather chair before his gleaming mahogany desk and then, before she even had a chance to drop her bit of bad news, he had pulled out the news clippings and waved them in front of her face.

'Forgive me for being paternalistic,' he went on, 'but I can't help being concerned about what you're doing to yourself. The last time we talked about Masters you were going to have him out in a few days. Now he's been there almost two weeks and the whole world knows about it.'

'He won't stay much longer,' she said.

Daniel gave her an ironic glance. 'Can you be specific?'

Jessica shook her head. The date she had fixed so determinedly for Philip's departure had crumbled, but she couldn't explain the reason to Daniel. He would never understand that Mrs Stanford's revelation about her father's heart attack and Philip's statement that she had kept him out of the hospital had shaken all of Jessica's bearings on the past to the point that she no longer cared about the future. She had once thought of her past as a mirror, clean and clear, that reflected the woman she had become, but now it was no longer so distinct and her image was blurring, the outlines wavering and shaky. The sequence of events, the causes and effects, were not as simple as she had supposed. There were things she had known nothing about and, even worse, things she either no longer remembered or had deliberately suppressed.

'No,' she said. 'I can't really say when he'll go.'

Daniel leaned back in his black leather, winged chair and looked grim. 'Be honest with me, Jess.'

'I'm always honest with you,' she replied, startled by his intensity.

'Are you sleeping with him?'

Her brown eyes were wide and shocked. 'Of course not!'

It was quite obvious that Jessica was telling the truth and Daniel sighed, half in relief, half in exasperation. 'Then I can only say that I think you've lost your senses.'

'The publicity will die down.'

He made a grimace. 'Maybe.'

'You know how reporters are; they'll lose interest when nothing happens.'

'Well, don't get distracted by it. Keep on with the book.'

Jessica swallowed. 'That's what I came by to talk about, Dan.'

Daniel put each forefinger to a temple, closed his eyes and pretended to be a swami. 'Don't tell me—I see in the crystal ball that it's not going well.'

'I can't seem to get into it. I don't know where to begin. I don't know the first thing . . .'

Daniel leaned forward. 'Admit that I'm justified in being disturbed, Jess. I've never known you to have writer's block before.'

'Maybe I was wrong in *All's Fair*. Maybe my theories about men are all off.'

'What kind of blarney has Masters been feeding you?' Daniel demanded angrily.

Jessica shook her head helplessly. 'Nothing.'

'Has he read your books?'

'Yes, but . . .'

'And he doesn't agree with them, I imagine.'

'Philip hasn't said much about . . .'

Daniel slapped his hand down on his leather blotter. 'It hurts. It really hurts, Jess, to see you turning from a confident professional into a quivering mass of insecurity because of Masters. His opinions about your work are irrelevant, his personality is obviously destructive and you're letting him have a power over you that is hardly warranted by any kind of relationship. Get rid of him! Kick him out of your house and give yourself a chance to settle down and think. Your publicity tour was hectic and no one expects you to . . .'

'I can't do the book. I . . . I'm sorry.'

Daniel stood up impatiently, pushing back his chair until it hit the bookcase behind his desk with a sound that made Jessica wince. He walked over to his window and stared out towards the horizon, his back to Jessica, his shoulders hunched forward, his hands jammed into the pockets of his grey suit. For a minute there was silence and then he spoke, his face still turned away.

'I've watched you grow,' he said slowly. 'When you first came to me you were frightened, easily intimidated

and unsure of yourself. Perhaps you can't see the
changes the way I can, but it's been one of the most
rewarding experiences of my life watching you develop.
You're a woman whose beauty has been enhanced by
serenity and confidence—you carry yourself well; you
hold your head up high; and you look like the success
that you are. Part of that comes from knowing yourself,
knowing your own strengths and weaknesses. What I
can't stand now is watching you become so uncertain
and lost about yourself because Masters has decided to
come back and marry you.' He turned then to face her.
'That is why he's here, isn't it?'

Jessica looked away from Daniel's direct blue gaze.
'Yes.'

'And?' he asked.

'No.' She shook her head vehemently. 'I don't ever
want to marry again.'

Daniel gave a slight smile. 'It isn't so bad, you know.
Not if two people are compatible. Margaret and I were
very happy together.'

Jessica was surprised at Daniel's mention of his wife.
He rarely talked about her and she had always assumed
that his reticence was tied to unhappy memories and grief;
Margaret Gilbert had died after a long and painful battle
with cancer five years earlier. Jessica realised that she
knew very little about Daniel when she put her mind to it.
She'd met his daughter, Annie, and had attended several
cocktail parties in his home in northern Virginia, but she
had certainly never been his confidante and she had no
real idea what he did when he wasn't talking to her on the
phone, meeting with her in his office or taking her out to
elegant restaurants for lunch.

'I've been burnt,' she said, 'and I'm twice shy.'

'Then why is he still with you?'

'Because . . .' she hesitated and then went on, 'I feel
sorry for him.'

'Come on, Jess,' he said impatiently. 'Be honest with
yourself.'

'I am,' she protested. 'He's hurt and he can't . . .'

'If you're not sleeping with him; if you're not going to marry him, then why the hell is he still in your house.'

Daniel's grim insistence made Jessica fumble with her words. 'He . . . I didn't understand everything . . . things happened during our marriage that . . .'

'Jessica.' Daniel walked over to the chair next to hers and, after sitting down in it, reached over and took her hand between his broad palms. 'Your fingers are like ice.'

She watched him rub her hand, his fingers short and wide and warm. His fingernails were clean and manicured, and he wore a black onyx ring on his left hand. She had a sudden perception of what it would be like to go to bed with Daniel—he would be loving and warm, kind and considerate. He would treat her like a piece of Dresden china, fragile and delicate. Passion would be subdued, the sheets would be only slightly rumpled, and the lights would be turned discreetly off.

'. . . I think you have to face the reasons why you're letting Masters stay,' he was saying.

'It's pity,' she said.

'No. You're still attracted to him.'

Jessica bent her head so that Daniel couldn't see her face. Why was it so obvious? She had thought that her feelings were hidden, safe from the eyes of the world. She couldn't help what she felt for Philip; sex had been the initial attraction and, quite possibly, the only link that had held them together at all. She had been stunned to find that a spark of sensuality had remained despite the years of anger and the acrimony. Whenever she and Philip were in the same room, she wanted to touch him, to remember the places her fingers had lingered in the past; the hard line of his jaw, the deep indentation of his spine, his firm muscular waist.

'I can't help it,' she finally acknowledged, raising her head.

Daniel sat back in his chair as if he had won a battle, letting her hand go. 'All right,' he said bluntly. 'Get Masters out of your system in whatever way is necessary. I don't give a damn if you can't write the book right now; you have all the time in the world for that.'

'I didn't think you'd understand,' she said, relief flooding her. The pressure Daniel put on her to write was never overt or heavy but she knew that he wanted her to work; her efforts benefited both of them.

His smile was ironic and self-deprecating, his eyes resting on the smooth oval lines of her face. 'What I understand, Jess, is that you won't let any other man into your life until you get Masters out first.'

Jessica had never quite thought about Philip as a housemate type, but during the week that preceded their trip to New York for the baptism he more than aptly fitted the role. They lived in amiable harmony, a state that neither had achieved during their marriage. Philip went every day to physiotherapy where he exercised and worked out with weights under the supervision of a doctor. In the evenings, he often read and Jessica found it strange to come upon him sitting in the living room, absorbed in a book. He had never been much of a reader when they were married; she had been the one who buried herself in books—as much for escape as anything else.

They didn't discuss what he was reading; their conversations were strictly practical and confined to daily living. Jessica might enquire about dinner; Philip would offer to help make the salad. Jessica would say she was going out; Philip would ask her to pick up some shaving cream. They might talk about mutual acquaintances or the fact that it was unusually warm for April. They were polite, restrained and considerate of one another. Philip gave her a cheque for his half of the house expenses and Jessica often drove him to the physiotherapist's office. The days slid by, the constraint between them as secure as a bolted and latched door. If Philip felt anything more than a friendly interest in Jessica, it wasn't noticeable to her, and his offer of marriage and his invitation to take her to bed seemed to have occurred in another time zone, on another planet.

Jessica used the tranquillity to begin a chore that she hadn't been able to face since moving into the house. She spring-cleaned on a vast scale, emptying out closets and piling box upon box of unwanted items in the garage. She got rid of all sorts of things; a cracked set of dishes, the bicycle she had ridden during junior high school, curtains that her mother had inherited from an elderly aunt, clothes that had gone out of style, an ancient vacuum cleaner, two ghastly ceramic lamps.

She found the accumulated memorabilia of thirty years gathering dust in an attic. It was all hers to do with as she wished since her parents had moved into a condominium in Florida with half the floor space of the house and virtually no place for relics of the past. She found her father's university degrees and her mother's teaching manuals. Sports equipment tumbled out of one box, including a first baseman's mitt and a bat which dated back to the year that Ben had decided to teach Jessica how to play baseball. She found a large plastic bag full of odds and ends of yarn from Dagmar's craft days and, hidden in one corner, under several garment bags of old coats, she discovered a box of photograph albums.

Some belonged to her grandmother's era; faded snapshots of women in dresses of coloured prints, their hair marceled and bobbed. She came upon a picture of her father at age four or five dressed in short pants and bow tie, his father behind him, stern and bearded. Jessica hadn't seen the albums since years earlier when she used to pore over them when she was home sick from school and, now fascinated with these glimpses of the past, she sat down on the splintery bare floor boards of the attic, delving through the books while the dust rose from each one as she lifted it out in a puff of faint brown smoke.

Her life had been captured in static, happy moments. There were pictures of Jessica as an infant, grinning a toothless smile while being held in Dagmar's arms, toddling with an outstretched pudgy arm over to a Christmas tree laden with tinsel and hangings, setting out for her first day of school in a checked dress and black patent leather shoes, her hair combed into sprightly pigtails adorned with crisp bows. The Harleys had taken pictures of her, it seemed, at every available moment; the albums were full of Jessica living out her childhood, growing into adolescence, becoming a woman.

Jessica enjoyed the remembering so much that she turned each page eagerly, curious about what would come next. It was like re-reading a book she had loved or going to see a wonderful film again. She forgot her surroundings; the hardness of the floor, the faint chill in the uninsulated attic, the musty odour, and the disorder of boxes and bags around her. She was transported back into a past when life was much simpler, when every day dawned brightly and the only unhappiness might come from a childish squabble or a whim denied by usually indulgent parents.

So immersed was she in warm memories that, when she turned the page, the next picture made her jerk backwards as if cold water had been thrown into her face. She had not known that it was being taken and had never seen it before. If she had, Jessica knew that she would have destroyed it along with her wedding album and scrapbook full of clippings in one of the fits of black hatred that had come over her after Philip had left. The photo had been taken during the summer in the backyard of the house when the trees were in full foliage and Dagmar's garden was in bloom. The background was green with dots of floral colour; pink, white and gold; the foreground held the trunk of a tree and a hammock that swung by itself on a metal frame.

The couple in the picture were in bathing suits, their skin tanned, the sun glinting in their dark hair. They were lying together in the hammock, their balance so precarious that the man had one bare foot on the ground and his arms wrapped around the woman's waist. The woman was reclining half-across him, one arm around his neck, the fingers of the other hand curled in the hair on his chest. Her long black hair tumbled over her bare shoulders and she looked happy and content, laughing into his upturned face. Even from a distance, the photographer had caught the intimate bond between them, and it was obvious that they were lovers. The picture had been taken a week before her wedding, a light-hearted affair that had also taken place in her parents' backyard where a striped red and white tent had been erected and the lawn had been dotted with tables set with red cloths and centrepieces of carnations.

Jessica stared at the picture for a while and then slowly closed the album, hiding the laughing couple, pressing them beneath many pages. They didn't exist anymore, perhaps they never had. Their happiness had been so delicate and ephemeral that the slightest wind had blown it apart, the way white fluff from a dandelion scatters into the air with the tiniest shake of the hand. Their intimacy had broken on the sharp point of anger; they had learned to look on one another with hatred instead of love. It was best, she thought sadly, to put such pictures away, to forget they existed, to conceal them in a box in the attic. The past was gone, the emotions lost in time. Nothing remained but the present.

As Megan had said on the phone, she and Simon were in a state of role reversal. It was Simon who carried Sarah Jessalyn from room to room, gave her a bath and changed her diapers. He was, Megan confided to Jessica, absolutely besotted with the baby. Jessica thought it was rather sweet to see Simon, six foot three and husky, cradling the baby in his arms and talking to her as if she could understand every word he said. Philip, on the other hand, took to ribbing Simon unmercifully.

'How's the breastfeeding going?' he asked on the evening of their arrival in New York.

Simon, who had been jiggling Sarah Jessalyn on his knee, fell in with the fun. 'It's murder,' he said, 'when she's hungry every hour, but I do feel so fulfilled knowing that I'm giving her a healthy start . . .'

'Enough,' Megan said with a laugh. 'And pass her over. She probably is starving; she's sucking on her blanket.'

The four of them were sitting in the living room of Megan and Simon's apartment. Jessica and Philip had arrived earlier in the afternoon; a slow and exhausting trip that required the use of wheel chairs at both National and La Guardia airports. Philip hadn't wanted to use them and had insisted on walking with his crutches, but he still tired quickly and Jessica had finally insisted when she saw him go pale with pain when a porter, carrying some bags, jostled him in a hallway. His cast went above his knee, and he had been forced to sit sideways in the place, his leg jutting out into the aisle. Although he didn't say anything, the trip had obviously drained his energies and, when they arrived at the Thompsons', Philip excused himself and slept for nearly two hours. It was during that time that Megan and Jessica had had their heart-to-heart talk.

'Separate rooms?' Megan asked as they had lunch. 'Or a double bed?'

'I'm not sleeping with him,' Jessica replied.

Megan shook her head in disbelief. 'Honest to god, Jess, he's one of the most gorgeous men, I know. How can you resist?'

Jessica was curt. 'Easily.'

'And he's crazy about you.'

'That's a myth of your own making, Meg.'

Megan took a bite of her sandwich and fixed Jessica with a stern look. 'For someone who's so smart, I can't figure out why you're acting so obtuse. Why would Philip come back to you if he didn't love you?'

Jessica shrugged. 'He's sick, he's at a loose end, he needs a woman, he wants to be a success at something he failed at before—there's half a dozen reasons why he's suddenly turned up out of the blue.'

'Why haven't you told him to leave then?'

'I feel sorry for him.'

'Philip doesn't strike me as the kind of man you feel sorry for,' Megan said shrewdly. 'If he thought you were keeping him out of pity, he'd have left weeks ago.'

Jessica picked at her salad. 'I can't speak for Philip,' she said.

'Jess,' Megan reached across the table and touched her hand, 'what's really going on? You look miserable.'

It was too complicated and too confusing to explain; Jessica wasn't sure that she understood it herself. She had the feeling that she was living in limbo, in some sort of blank space where time stood still. In one direction was the future, a closed door and, in the other direction, was a door that was barely open, the dark sliver inviting her to enter, to investigate the uncertainties and ambiguities of her past. Philip might be the key to that past and she no longer wanted him to leave. She saw his presence as the means to an end, as a connection to past events, as an interpreter of the truth, but it was a belief that was far too hard to communicate in Megan's sunny kitchen where copper pots hung on the white walls and a kettle whistled on the stove.

'When I figure it out, I'll let you know,' she had said and Megan, with a sympathetic glance, had nodded and then gone on to discuss Sarah Jessalyn's feeding schedule with all the enthusiasm of a new mother.

Now, as she sat on the couch watching Megan nurse her daughter, Jessica felt envy curl within her. The baby was soft and sweet, the top of her head dotted with fine red curls, her eyes closed, one small fist patting Megan's breast as she sucked. The miscarriage had occurred so early in Jessica's pregnancy that she had never known whether she would have borne a boy or a girl, but it hadn't mattered at the time. Losing the baby had meant losing all the expectations that came with motherhood; the responsibilities, the joys, the worries and the delights. Jessica glanced at Philip and saw that he was watching Megan with a brooding look. She wondered if he was remembering how close he had brushed against fatherhood.

'It's a miracle,' Simon was saying as he watched his wife and daughter. He looked tired but happy, a sandy-haired giant with warm brown eyes and a nose that had once been broken by a fall from his bicycle at age fifteen and hadn't been straight since. 'Fifteen minutes of pleasure and look what you end up with.'

Megan winked at them. 'Simon's been using a stop watch.'

Philip grinned. 'Trying out for a competition, Simon?'

Megan intervened. 'You know how executives are—businesslike. Turn off the lights, pull down the sheets . . .'

'Megan,' Simon warned, 'be serious and watch your language. You're a mother now.'

'I plan to be just as outrageous as I ever was. Sarah Jessalyn needs an interesting mother, don't you?' She pulled the baby away from her breast, making a face at her, and then closed the opening in her blouse with efficiency. 'Take breastfeeding in public for instance. Simon's mother can't stand it.'

'My mother was brought up in another era.'

Megan brought Sarah Jessalyn up to her shoulder and energetically patted her tiny back. 'Mmmm—burp, baby, or you'll get colicky again. Let's face it, Simon, your mother thinks I'm a bit *risqué* and not right for her son.'

Simon was about to speak when Philip leaned over from his chair and put his arms out. 'Can I hold her?' he asked Megan.

She gave him a surprised look. 'You want the baby?'

'Why not?' he asked. 'I promise not to drop her.'

Megan raised her eyebrows at Jessica but, cupping Sarah Jessalyn's head in her hand, she passed her to Philip. The baby, who had been sleeping, yawned once—a cavernous, gum-filled yawn—and then went back to sleep again. She lay nestled in Philip's arms, a small feminine bundle in a pink-sprigged nightgown, the colour bright against the black of his slacks and turtleneck. Jessica couldn't help the catch in her throat when she watched Philip bend his dark head over the baby as he tucked her up to his chest.

'She's been known to get damp,' Simon warned.

'We've thought of putting a buzzer in her diaper,' Megan added.

'I don't mind,' Philip said with a lazy smile.

'It's hard to imagine you as a father,' Megan said.

'Maybe I just need practise.'

Simon pursed his mouth into a small whistle and gave Jessica a high sign. 'Is there something you want to tell us, Philip?'

'Nope.'

'No plans for the future?'

'Not that I know of.'

'No playmates for Sarah Jessalyn?'

Philip shook his head. 'I just like babies.'

The catch in Jessica's throat threatened to shatter into a thousand, painfully jagged pieces. *Since when?* she wanted to cry out. *Since when have you liked babies?* The Philip she had known hadn't cared about children in the least. He had never wanted any and had told her in no uncertain terms that he wouldn't consider being a father himself. And then when she had got pregnant and when he had found out, he had . . . Jessica suddenly felt the tears behind her eyes and she stood up, knocking her shin against the coffee table and almost overturning a tray of drinks.

'Are you all right?' Megan asked hurriedly when she saw Jessica's face.

'Just tired. I think I'll go to bed.' She kept her eyes averted from Philip; she didn't want him to see her distress.

'I guess we should all go to bed,' Simon said. 'The baptism is at ten o'clock tomorrow.'

Megan made a grimace. 'And don't forget to pray,' she added, 'that Sarah Jessalyn doesn't make fools out of all of us.'

But the baby couldn't have been better, and they were later to joke that she must have known that she was in a church where silence and clean diapers were sacrosanct. She lay quietly in Jessica's arms as the minister spoke, her dark blue eyes fixed nowhere in particular, only flinching slightly when the baptismal water was dropped on her small forehead. She was dressed in a long white gown with yards of lace trimming and tiny, satin booties with lace ties. A frilly cap hid her red curls and framed the circle of her face. Even at three weeks, it was obvious who Sarah Jessalyn was going to look like and, if the origin of the red hair was a mystery, the nose and mouth were strictly Megan's, a resemblance that didn't sit well with Simon's mother.

'Can't see a bit of Simon in that child,' Mrs Thompson said to Jessica at the luncheon that Megan had after the ceremony. She was a petite woman with blue-rinsed curls, narrow grey eyes and an unhappy mouth. Jessica always remembered Megan saying that her mother-in-law should never have outlived Simon's father. Widowhood had soured her on life.

'Perhaps she'll have Simon's temperament,' Jessica replied tactfully.

'One would hope,' the older woman replied with asperity. 'Megan is extremely undisciplined.'

Jessica was thankful that they weren't in earshot of anyone. 'Meg isn't very neat,' she agreed and then added loyally, 'but she's a wonderful person.'

'I mean undisciplined in regards to her mind. She can't seem to buckle down to anything.'

Jessica glanced at Megan who was busy talking to one of Simon's sisters. 'She designs dresses,' she said. 'In fact, I think she's wearing one of her own.' She had admired Megan's outfit earlier, a dark blue suit with a side-pleated skirt and a jacket without lapels. Megan's figure had returned with an astonishing rapidity; the only discernible difference was that she was more voluptuous than ever.

Mrs Thompson shook her head, her mouth pursed into a disapproving line. 'I don't mean dress designing; I mean family responsibilities. Simon's father was a philanthropist and Simon is expected to follow in his footsteps. His wife has certain duties and a position to maintain. Megan, I'm afraid, prefers to ignore them.'

Jessica changed the subject and finally managed to slip away from Mrs Thompson with a feeling of relief and a sudden empathy with Megan who complained about her mother-in-law frequently and vociferously, calling her eccentric, strait-laced and irritating. Megan had always scoffed at Simon's family and what she termed their 'social pretensions', and Jessica had been sympathetic, understanding that Megan wouldn't be caught dead at a charity ball or afternoon tea, dressed to the hilt and conversing politely with strangers. It simply wasn't her style and Simon had known when he married her that his choice of wife ran counter to the family grain. Still, the clash of culture and life-style had had its after effects and Jessica, who saw Megan and Simon as the ideal couple, was forced to admit that even a marriage with money, love and all the advantages in the world could have its problems.

An old college friend that she hadn't seen in years came up to say hello and Jessica forgot all about Megan's problems. The luncheon ended around two o'clock, and everyone breathed a sigh of relief as the last guest departed. Megan claimed exhaustion and went to bed after handing Sarah Jessalyn over to the nanny while Philip and Simon closeted themselves in the study. Jessica left for an appointment with the publisher who had picked up the paperback option on *All's Fair* and spent an exhausting and probably futile afternoon with their marketing manager trying to convince him that the mushroom cloud that had appeared on the hardcover copies was in excessively bad taste and hadn't, as far as she was concerned, sold one extra copy.

They then went for dinner with a group of Megan and Simon's friends in a fancy restaurant in mid-town Manhattan and came home late to find the nanny who had stayed to babysit walking a fussy Sarah Jessalyn up and down the long central hallway of the apartment. Simon immediately took the baby into his arms and gave the nanny a frowning inquisition.

'Have you changed her diaper?' he asked and Mrs Dibbern, round, plump and a nanny to many babies, merely nodded soothingly.

'She's as clean as a whistle.'

Simon rocked a whimpering Sarah Jessalyn and gave the nanny a disbelieving look. 'Did you give her some water? Didn't she want the pacifier?'

Mrs Dibbern was obviously accustomed to the intense anxieties of new fathers. 'Now, it's just a bit of colic, Mr Thompson,' she said as she pulled on her coat. 'There's not a thing to worry about.'

Simon was already marching Sarah Jessalyn down the hallway to the nursery, patting her tiny back and trying to talk some sense into her. 'Come on, sweetie pie,' he murmured. 'Daddy's home now. Everything's going to be all right.'

Megan threw Jessica and Philip a can-you-believe-it look as she headed after them. 'Sometimes I get the feeling I'm redundant,' she said. 'If I weren't the baby's source of food, the two of them wouldn't need me at all.'

Philip and Jessica exchanged smiles as they went into their prospective bedrooms and Jessica crawled thankfully between the covers of her bed. She was tired from the day and admittedly thankful at the moment that Sarah Jessalyn wasn't her responsibility. She and Philip were leaving tomorrow and she needed a good night's sleep to face the trip back to Washington. She had a suspicion that Philip wasn't looking forward to it either, but they'd hardly talked since their arrival in Manhattan. He'd spent most of his time with Simon.

It was the voices that woke her; they were so loud that she could hear them all the way down at her end of the apartment. She blinked into the darkness, tried to turn over and go back to sleep again and then finally gave up in defeat. The voices were too loud, too abrasive and too shrill despite her closed door, and Jessica couldn't hide from them, much as she would have liked to. It sounded very much like Megan and Simon were in the midst of a rousing battle and she really didn't want to hear the things that they were saying to one another. She tried to cover her head with the pillow and then to cover her ears with her hands, but it was impossible to stay in either position for very long and she finally sat up and, switching on the light, tried to read a magazine. When that didn't work, she decided to visit the bathroom. If she ran the shower, she wouldn't be able to hear a thing.

Opening her door meant letting the accusations and anger right into her bedroom and Jessica winced as she listened to Megan screaming.

'I'd like to know why the hell you married me. Your mother can't stand me, your sister is a snob and your brother is a damned stuffed shirt!'

Simon's voice was a rumble in the distance and then Megan spoke again, 'I don't care who she is, she can't dictate my life. I absolutely refuse to be dragged around to her social life. They're all a bunch of lousy hypocrites—you know that?'

'You could try to understand and be a bit accommodating.'

'She doesn't understand me! She doesn't give a damn about what I think or care about it. She's always been like that—from the day we got married, she's thought of me as the enemy who snatched away her golden-haired boy and ruined him.'

Simon's voice was cold. 'And what about you? You had your back up the moment you met her.'

'She's a bitch, Simon, why don't you admit it? Even you don't like her!'

'I'm sick and tired of fighting with you about my mother. Either you learn to live with her or . . .'

'Or what, Simon?' Megan's voice was taunting. 'Do you want me to leave or would you kick me out instead?'

Jessica found she was trembling and she wrapped her arms around her, hugging the thin fabric of her nightgown against her skin. It wasn't cold in the apartment but the atmosphere was chilling. It scared her that Megan and Simon could fight like this. It threw all her beliefs about their marriage into jeopardy. She had thought that they loved one another, that they cared about one another, that their marriage was as solid as a rock.

The voices began again and Jessica crept down the hallway, her feet bare and cold against the polished wood. She'd spend the night in the bathroom if it meant that she could get away from them. She couldn't bear the pain that she was hearing or the anger that vibrated in the air. It reminded her too much of her own fights with Philip, those earth-shaking battles when she would go hoarse from screaming and he would be as cold as ice.

She put her hands over her ears and moved faster, trying to slip past Philip's door when it suddenly opened and his hand pinioned her wrist. 'Come in here,' he said in a low voice, 'and close the door behind you.'

CHAPTER SIX

THE lamp by the bed had been turned on, sending a soft yellow glow over the bed with its creamy white and rust spread. Philip had not yet gone to sleep; he was still dressed in grey slacks and a white shirt, but his jacket had been thrown over the back of a chair and his tie had been loosened, revealing the tanned and muscular hollow of his throat. The bed bore the imprint of his body where he had been lying and reading. Folders and looseleaf binders lay in a pile beside the night table and the radio gave off a low sound of instrumental music.

Jessica closed the door as Philip skilfully manouevred himself back to the bed and, placing his crutches against the wall, stretched out on the covers, his back propped up against the headboard. Not even the bulky weight of his cast marred the long length of his legs or the tapered line of his hips, and Jessica stood uncertainly by the door jamb, suddenly aware of her hair which hung loose and tangled to her shoulders and the transparency of her white nightgown which, although it covered her from neck to toes, revealed the lines of her body wherever it touched her skin.

Philip gestured to a rust-coloured corduroy chair. 'Sit down,' he said. 'You look like a gothic heroine about to be seduced.'

As Jessica obeyed him, Simon's voice came loud and clear through the closed door and she reacted visibly, drawing her bare feet up under her and wrapping her arms over her knees. 'It's terrible,' she said.

'Woke you up?'

'That isn't what bothers me. It's the fighting; I had no idea that Simon and Megan were like this.'

'Like what?'

'At one another's throat. I . . . thought that they were so close.'

'What makes you think that they aren't?'

Jessica gave him a disbelieving look. 'They're angry; they're saying horrible things to each other.'

The gleam of the lamp was caught in the bronzed skin of Philip's cheekbone and lean line of jaw as he leaned forward. 'You never did like fighting, Jess.'

'Of course I didn't! It's upsetting and destructive.'

'Not always.'

'In our case . . .'

'In our case it was, but Megan and Simon will survive.'

There was another spate of loud voices and Jessica shook her head. 'I don't know how you can say that. Listen to them!'

'It's their way of working out their problems.'

'Or heading towards a divorce.'

Philip loosened his tie completely and pulled it off from his neck. 'They won't divorce over Simon's mother. They're just airing their differences and letting off steam. Simon knows Meg has a strong personality and he knew when he married her that she'd never get along with his mother, but it didn't matter to him particularly. He adores Meg's flamboyance. He knows he'd be a stick in the mud without her.'

'But they're screaming at each other!'

Philip's mouth set in a line of impatience. 'The trouble with you, Jess, is that you don't know the first thing about fighting. You weren't very good at it.'

Now he was picking at her again. 'And you were perfect at it, I suppose,' she said sarcastically.

'No, I wasn't much good at it either. I think it's a skill that has to be learned in childhood and neither of us had any examples to fall back on. Your parents didn't fight at all and mine never stopped.'

'Your parents,' she said pointedly, 'didn't love one another.'

His mouth twisted at the reminder. 'My parents hated each other,' he said. 'It's a wonder their marriage lasted as long as it did. They had fifteen years of accusations and recriminations, fighting over every issue from the state of the bank account to the way I acted at the dinner table.' There was a brief moment of silence and Philip threw his arm over his eyes as if he could erase the images he was seeing. Then his voice continued, the words clipped and precise, 'There were times that I wanted to die then, times that I thought if I were dead, then they'd be happy.'

Philip had never talked much about his childhood other than to express a few bitter sentiments, and Jessica clenched her hands together because she too could envision a small boy caught in the middle of his parents' wrath; vulnerable, helpless and frightened. 'You weren't the cause of your parents' divorce,' she said softly.

He brought his arm down and sighed. 'Oh, I know it now. They were mismatched and miserable and my presence was a constant reminder of the mistakes they had made. I was the product of an unwanted pregnancy and a shotgun wedding.'

Jessica leaned forward, intent on making him see it from her perspective. 'My parents married for love,' she said. 'They didn't fight because they cared too much to allow minor disagreements to come between them.'

He gave her a sharp metallic glance. 'You parents didn't fight because they didn't give a damn about each other. They had a terminal case of indifference.'

Jessica began to get off the chair. 'I think we've been over this ground before.'

'And one of the problems with our marriage was that you were aiming for a duplicate case of the blahs.'

'I told you,' she hissed. 'My parents cared deeply about their marriage.'

Philip shook his head as if in admiration of her stubbornness. 'You never could give up your cosy little myths.'

'They're not myths!'

He grabbed her wrist as she swept by the bed and pulled her down beside him. Jessica had no choice but to submit; his grasp was so strong that she couldn't wiggle out of it, and their shoulders met, his face so close to hers that she could see the individual dark lashes that framed his silvery eyes. She caught the scent of his aftershave, a tangy pleasant male smell that made her shiver slightly, and she pulled away from him as far as she could go, not liking to be too close. Proximity to Philip made her heart jolt and then race and she knew that the rapid rise and fall of her breasts could be seen beneath her nightgown.

'You should wear your hair down,' he said softly, running his fingers through the tangled strands at her temple. 'It becomes you.'

Jessica tried to pull her head back. 'I prefer it up. It's more practical.'

'Oh, Jess,' he said with a note of sadness in his voice. 'You've become hard.'

The insult stung. 'You made me that way,' she said coldly.

'How?'

Jessica almost answered with a flip, evasive remark but something in his expression stopped her. 'By ... pushing me away when we were married,' she admitted slowly, 'by showing me that you didn't want my affection.'

Philip was silent for a second, his gaze steady on her flushed face. 'Guilty as charged.'

Jessica stared at him and then looked down at his hand which still pinioned her wrist, surprised and startled that he would agree with her so readily. She had accused him of the same thing three years ago and he had retaliated by calling her a child.

'So you admit it,' she said.

'Yes, but you asked for more than any man could give.'

'I didn't,' she said hotly.

'You wanted the same relationship with me that you had with your father.'

'I wanted a husband, not a father!'

'Jess,' his hand left her wrist and cupped the smooth curve of her cheek, 'I don't think you knew the difference then.'

She was almost too bemused by his touch on her face to think. 'You're accusing me . . .' she began.

'I'm not accusing you of anything,' he said gently. 'You were young and immature and very, very desirable.'

The kiss didn't come as a surprise; everything had led up to it: the pool of golden light on the bed, the darkness in the corners of the room, the absolute stillness in the rest of the apartment. It seemed as if the bed were the centre of the universe and they were the only people in it. Philip pulled her down slowly, his hand on her shoulder, pressing her back against the pillows. Her breasts brushed against the side of his chest, their hips touched, her leg ran the length of his. Their lips met in a gentle touching, and then moved to their tongues, meeting and exploring in the corners of their mouths and then moving inwards. It was sweeter than Jessica's memories and sweeter than all her imaginings. She closed her eyes and leaned back into the curve of Philip's arm, her fingers rising to brush inside the open collar of his shirt where a steady pulse beat in his throat.

'You taste better than I remember,' Philip said huskily, burying his face against her neck.

'I . . . I'm not ready for this,' she replied, her voice shaky.

'I know,' he murmured, 'but I couldn't help it.'

She felt the softness of his mouth against the skin under her earlobe and then a flick of his tongue. 'No?' she asked softly.

He lifted his head and smiled down at her. 'If you

need to know how much I want you, touch me and find out.'

'And risk rape?' she teased.

'I'd prefer to think of it as a coordinated effort.' He leaned forward and brushed her lips with his mouth.

'Philip?'

'Mmmm?'

'Did you mean it when you said that you'd been wrong, too?'

'I didn't know how to handle your emotions. You were so intense.'

'I just wanted us to have a normal marriage . . .'

'You weren't realistic, Jess, and we didn't fit into your idea of the perfect marriage. You wanted a rose-covered cottage and a husband with a nine to five job who would leave in the morning with his briefcase in his hand and return in the evening to appreciate your cooking.'

She stiffened in his arms. 'You're not being fair. I was a bit more liberated than that.'

'Not much.' The words were said without rancour and his silvery eyes were gleaming at her, amused and tender.

Jessica glanced away, unable to bear the sudden surge of her own emotions. Philip's honesty had disarmed her and left her without any defences, his kiss had opened a floodgate of barely remembered sensations and his hand, which rested lightly at her waist, was stroking her skin through the fabric of her nightgown, causing a warmth to move within her and a slow tightening of her stomach muscles. Jessica knew that contraction as the first signal of desire, the first physical response to an emotion that her mind had acknowledged when she had seen Philip sleeping in her bed three weeks ago. Her own sensuality, unleashed and liberated, was moving through her veins, pulsing ahead with every quick beat of her heart and filling her breasts until her nipples rose to points so sensitive that even the soft touch of the delicate cotton resting over them caused her a pleasurable agony.

'I think I'd better go,' she said, backing out of Philip's arms.

'Do you?' His voice caressed her.

'Philip, I don't want . . .'

He let go of her, but with one hand he picked up a long silky strand of hair from her shoulder and ran his mouth down its black length. 'I know,' he said softly. 'You'll come to me when you want to. I can wait until then.'

The Harleys arrived in Washington two days later during an afternoon when Philip was visiting the physiotherapist. Jessica picked them up at the airport and brought them back to the house where they sat in the living room, opened their suitcases and poured out the contents, a seemingly never-ending supply of gifts and purchases from the Greek islands. Ben had turned into an amateur archeological expert on Hellenic ruins, and Dagmar had a new wardrobe of embroidered shirts, beautifully knitted sweaters and loosely cling-ing dresses that reminded Jessica of the robes she had seen on sculptures of Greek goddesses. Her parents looked so tanned and so happy that Jessica discarded everything that Philip had said about them. He couldn't have been more wrong, she decided, as she listened to them talk and watched their animated faces. There was an affection between them and an understanding that would have been evident to anyone.

'And your father bought every guidebook he could get his hands on,' Dagmar was saying in loving exasperation. 'We could have used an extra suitcase for all his books.'

Ben laughed and leaned expansively back against the couch he was sharing with Jessica. 'And your mother had an attraction for the jewelry stores. I kept having to

remind her that there was a limit to how many things
we could bring back.'

They were relaxed with one another; Jessica could see
that. Her mother was lively and vivacious, her brown
hair only slightly streaked with grey, her figure in the
beige sheath, still slim for a woman in her mid-fifties.
Dagmar dressed well and made the most of herself;
she had always been an expert with make-up and kept
her hair in a flattering soft halo around her face. Age
had treated her well as it had Ben. He was still
distinguished-looking and his new tan made his hair
seem even more silver in contrast. Jessica had always
been proud of her resemblance to her father; they were
both tall and shared the same high cheekbones and
slightly cleft chin. As a child, she had assumed that the
resemblance gave them an extra element of closeness, a
certain affinity for one another that went beyond
anything Dagmar could understand.

Now as she watched Ben smile, Jessica found that she
couldn't so easily shrug off Philip's intimations about
her relationship with her father as she had his
statements concerning her parents' marriage. She had
always preferred Ben to Dagmar; they'd been buddies,
friends and confidantes during all the years of her
childhood and adolescence. It wasn't that she and
Dagmar fought or hadn't got along; it was simply, she
had always understood, a matter of personalities. But
now she perceived of her closeness to Ben in a different
light. Had she been too attached to her father? And had
that attachment been so strong that it had interfered
with her marriage?

She shook the thought off as Ben spoke, 'And what
about you, Jess? How are the books doing?'

'Very well.'

'How many weeks on the bestseller list?'

'Ten.'

'How about fabulously well?' Dagmar asked with a
smile.

Jessica gave a self-deprecating shrug. 'Better than Dan and I expected,' she responded.

Ben gave Dagmar a grin. 'Have you ever noticed how modest our only child can be. Listen, honey, we're so proud of you that we could bust.'

Dagmar rolled her eyes expressively. 'Your father told everyone we met about you. He showed your picture to perfect strangers.' She mimed Ben flipping open his wallet and displaying Jessica's photograph. '"My daughter, Jessica Harley, author of two best-sellers, *Lost Souls* and *All's Fair*. Never heard of them? Then perhaps you'll recognise her. She's been on television."'

Jessica gave Ben a look of reproach. 'Daddy, you didn't.'

'And why not?' he asked with an air of mock-belligerence as he put his arm around Jessica and hugged her tightly. 'I love you and want to show you off. In fact, I'm dying to know what you're working on now so I can brag to my friends about the next bestseller.'

Jessica pulled herself out of the curve of his arm. 'I'm afraid that I'm not actually working on any book right now.'

'I thought you were doing research on unwed mothers,' said Dagmar.

'I was ... I thought I'd like to, but unfortunately, I ...' she faltered.

Ben threw Dagmar a look of concern. 'Honey, you can tell us if there's something wrong.'

Jessica couldn't look at either of her parents. Instead, she glanced down at her lap where her fingers were twining together in nervous apprehension. 'He isn't here right now ...' she began.

She felt Ben's fingers tighten on her shoulder. 'You're living with someone?'

Jessica quickly shook her head. 'No, he's just visiting.'

Dagmar leaned forward. 'Who's visiting, Jess?'

'Philip ... He's staying with me for a while. He ... he was hurt in a racing accident.'

She missed the look that passed between Ben and Dagmar, a conspiratorial look that hinted at knowledge and complicity. When she did raise her head, her mother simply said, 'How nice to see Philip again.'

Ben lifted his hand off Jessica's shoulder as he added, 'I heard about the accident before we left for Greece.'

'I suppose it will be the end of racing for him,' Dagmar went on, 'but then I had the feeling that he wanted to change careers, didn't you, Ben?'

'Racing is hard on the nerves,' her father agreed. 'It isn't the sort of thing that a man can do for his entire life.'

'And Philip had nerves of steel, but I think that even those began to fray around the edges.'

'It isn't something I could do,' Ben acknowledged. 'I was never into speed myself.'

Dagmar suddenly clapped her hands together in delight. 'Remember that taxi driver in Rhodes, Ben, the one who drove us to the hotel. My God, you went absolutely white!'

Ben began to laugh in return as they went into a reminiscence and Jessica sat in wide-eyed astonishment, glancing from one parent to another. Didn't they care that Philip had returned? Didn't they wonder about her relationship with him? She could recall quite vividly Ben's feelings after she had lost the baby. His distress for her had been obvious, and his anger and disgust with Philip had been vehement and vocal. Both her parents had pulled her back under their wing at the dissolution of her marriage, and she had never doubted that they were on her side. They had never actually blamed Philip in words, but Jessica had always known that Ben and Dagmar considered him the guilty party.

But now, it seemed as if they held Philip's momentous re-entry into her life as insignificant and

unimportant. They were far more interested in
rehashing their vacation adventures, and Jessica felt a
sudden sensation of abandonment, followed by a flush of
anger. She wanted to stand up and scream, *Look at me!
Listen to me!* I'm miserable, unhappy and confused.
Philip wants to marry me again and I don't know how I
feel about him. He's changed my past and I'm scared of
the future. I thought I'd healed from the marriage and
losing the baby but I haven't; he's touched me in places
where I'm raw, exposed and vulnerable and it hurts so
much that sometimes I can't stand the pain. Can't you see
that I'm frightened and shivering inside? Don't you care
how much I'm suffering? I thought you loved me!

But, of course, Jessica did nothing of the sort. She sat
there and smiled indulgently as if her parents were the
children and she were the adult. She even laughed a bit
as her father recounted a humorous story, and her
performance must have been convincing because her
parents acted as if her behaviour was as normal as
apple pie. It came to her, in a painful realisation, that
she had no right to inflict her own problems on anyone,
her parents included. If she voiced her fears, she would
wipe the happiness from their faces, steal this moment
of joy from them, and Jessica couldn't bring herself to
do that, no matter how much she wanted their
sympathy and support.

Growing up, Jessica now saw, meant freeing the
people you loved from burdens that they couldn't carry
and problems they couldn't solve. In the past she had
looked automatically to Ben and Dagmar for help
whenever she hurt, emotionally and physically. It was a
link that had been forged during her infancy and
childhood, and she had clung to it even into her
twenties, never realising that she had reciprocated her
parents' love and generosity with a self-centred and
egotistical desire to ease her concerns by passing them
on to someone else.

Understanding her selfish dependancy was painful

enough, but acting to remedy her behaviour was even worse. During the next few days, Jessica was forced to maintain a smiling silence that took every ounce of strength that she possessed. Her parents treated Philip almost as if he were a son. Dagmar chatted to him about travelling, books, movies and gardening. Ben challenged him to an on-going game of chess that they alternated with deep conversations about corporate law. There were times when she watched Philip and her parents talk, joke and laugh together that Jessica's resolution wavered and stumbled, and she longed to throw herself into Ben's arms and ask for the comforting she'd got as a child. The only thing that held her back and kept the smile pasted on her face was the knowledge that Ben couldn't traverse the dark territory that lay between Philip and herself. It was theirs alone; an uncharted, unexplored expanse of pain and love, of hurt and happiness, of isolation and incredible moments of intimacy.

Still, it bothered her to see Dagmar being solicitous of Philip's injury and to watch Ben treat him with affection. She had always known that her parents liked Philip, but she'd thought the feeling had evaporated during her divorce. Now she wondered if she hadn't grafted her own hatred of Philip on to her parents' emotions and falsely believed that it had taken root. Perhaps they had merely been diplomatic and sympathetic, knowing full well that there was nothing they could have said during the separation and divorce that would have convinced Jessica that Philip was anything but the bastard she had then called him.

The sight of Ben and Philip arguing with friendly vehemence about a chess move on the third day of her parents' visit finally drove Jessica out of the living room, and she wandered into the doorway of the screened porch where Dagmar was lying on a lounger and enjoying the sunlight that came pouring in through the budding trees.

For a second, Jessica watched her mother's delicate profile, reflecting on how pretty Dagmar still was and wondering with a sudden trace of bitterness where she herself would be at fifty-six. Unmarried with ten bestsellers about the human condition under her belt? A so-called 'expert' on marriage and the family while her own life was sterile and empty? Jessica caught her breath at the thought, appalled at the change she felt in herself. A month ago, she had wanted nothing more than the peace and serenity of her existence as a writer and as a single woman. She'd been envious of Megan's pregnancy, but it was an emotion she could push aside when she contemplated her own ambitions. Now, she foresaw a future as bleak as a moonscape because it didn't hold a man and children and she cringed inwardly. She'd always been contemptuous of women who couldn't envision life without a man.

'Jess, is that you?' Dagmar asked, her eyes closed against the sun.

'Yes. Mind if I join you?'

'Heavens, no. It's delightful out here. One of my big regrets about living in Florida is missing the Washington spring. It's so lovely.'

Jessica sat down in a webbed chair beside her mother and put her feet up on a glass coffee table. Although the sun was bright, the air was still cool and they were both dressed warmly, in wool slacks and turtleneck sweaters; Jessica in blue, Dagmar in camel and brown. A stranger watching them would never have guessed that they were mother and daughter. There was no resemblance between Dagmar's rounded, soft features and Jessica's unconscious hauteur, and their colouring was different. Dagmar's hair was light-brown, her eyes blue, her complexion fair. Jessica had Ben's dark, dramatic looks.

'Are you sorry that you moved?' Jessica asked.

Dagmar turned to her and blinked. 'No, I don't mean that at all. Your father and I needed a change of scenery. It's done us a world of good.'

Jessica took a deep breath. 'Why didn't you tell me that Dad had a heart attack?' she asked.

Dagmar gave her a quick glance. 'Who told you?'

'Mrs Stanford.'

'I told your father that you should know,' Dagmar said with a sigh, 'but he made me promise not to tell you.'

Jessica leaned towards her. 'But I wanted to know! I . . .' She threw her hands in the air in a gesture of complete exasperation.

'I know, dear, and I agree with you, but Ben was adamant. He recovered well and he didn't see any reason to worry you with his condition.'

'Mom, he retired because of it!'

'He retired for a lot of other reasons as well,' Dagmar said gently. 'The heart attack was just the final straw.'

'I'm not a child anymore,' Jessica insisted.

'I know and I told him that, but your father was always very protective of you. He couldn't bear to see you hurt or worried.'

Jessica had always known how Ben felt about her and she'd always relished the feeling he gave her of being special and unique, but now she saw the binds of his love as tight and suffocating, restrictive and limiting. For the very first time, she had a sudden inkling of the way Philip must have felt when they were married. She had unconsciously expressed her love for him the way Ben had taught her; by trying to take care of him and by trying to insulate him from the outside world. And she had expected the same love in return; she had even demanded it—an unconditional sort of love, the type of emotion a parent gives to a child; steady, all-encompassing and never judgmental.

'Is Dad okay now?' she asked with a resigned sigh.

Dagmar gave her a conspiratorial smile. 'He's doing just fine, but I keep an eye on his diet, make sure that he gets the right exercise and I don't let him get too involved in any one project. You know your father; he'd run the world if he could.'

Jessica recognised the moment as one she had been waiting for—a short time of intimacy with her mother that might not be achieved again. Cautiously, she asked, 'You said that there were other reasons why he had retired?'

Dagmar was quite willing to talk. 'The heart attack was just a symptom of a lot of other problems. He'd neglected so many things during the years that he worked. There were hobbies he wanted to pursue, places he wanted to go to, books he wanted to read. The heart attack made him stop for a moment and evaluate his life.'

Jessica took a deep breath. 'Did it change your marriage?'

Dagmar looked away for a second, staring at a cardinal that came to rest on the branch of a tree, his red-cocked head tilted, his tail quivering. His mate landed beside him, a brown bird; small, colourless and undistinguished, and the two of them perched companionably for a second, before flying off together, startled by some tiny sound or motion.

Finally she turned back to Jessica. 'You've never asked about our marriage before,' she said.

Jessica took a deep breath. 'Philip says that you stayed together because of me, that you and Dad really didn't care about one another.'

'I see.' Dagmar fingered the rings on her left hand, the broad gold wedding band and its matching diamond marquise.

'But now you seem so happy together that it doesn't make sense. Perhaps Philip is merely jealous because his family had so many problems. He had a rotten childhood and I didn't; I was so happy and . . .'

'Your father and I,' Dagmar began slowly, 'married very young and we believed that we were in love— madly, crazily in love. Perhaps it was infatuation;

perhaps it was a delusion; perhaps it was merely a case of puppy love, but whatever it was, it didn't last out the first year. By then I was pregnant with you and I couldn't envision divorce. That would have meant admitting to failure and I've always hated that.'

Suddenly, Jessica wasn't sure that she wanted to hear her mother's confession. She had a sick feeling that Philip had been right all along and that her past had shifted once more, revealing deeper crevasses and darker holes than before. 'Mom, I . . .'

Dagmar went on as if reciting a set piece, something that she had memorised if ever she were called upon to say it. 'We were friends, Ben and I, good friends and occasionally lovers. We drifted along for years and you were the focal point of our lives.' She stopped for a second, her voice breaking slightly. 'We were so proud of you, Jess. You were so beautiful and bright and showed so much promise that any unhappiness in our marriage seemed unimportant compared to what we wanted for you.'

Jessica could barely speak. 'All those years,' she whispered.

Dagmar gave a wry acknowledgement. 'Years when we drifted from one event to another, not miserable but not happy either. It wasn't until your father's heart attack that we began to talk about our marriage and what we wanted to do with the rest of our lives. We'd both contemplated leaving one another, but we discovered that we liked living together. We're good companions, Jess, and that counts for a lot. And then somewhere along the line, in the first year of Ben's retirement, we re-discovered love.' She gave a shaky little laugh. 'Passionate, sexy love, isn't that extraordinary?'

'You mean you and Dad . . .'

'Precisely.' Dagmar suddenly leaned over and took one of Jessica's hands. 'I fell in love with your father again, only this time it's the head over heels, true-blue variety. He's been a different man since he was sick; he's fun and interesting and charming. Now that he isn't so absorbed in his work, we've found so many things that we enjoy doing together.'

Jessica gripped her mother's hand. 'I think it's wonderful,' she said softly.

'You'll never know how I envied you, Jess.'

'Envied me?'

'Your relationship with Philip. When you came home before the wedding and I saw the way you looked at one another, I envied you that love and attraction. There was a spark between you so bright that I swore I could almost see it shining.'

Jessica pulled her hand away from her mother's soft grasp. 'Yes,' she said bitterly, 'there was.'

'And it's been interesting watching the two of you for the past few days.'

'Interesting!' Jessica would have called her relationship with Philip gut-wrenching perhaps, or heart-breaking or downright unhealthy, but never 'interesting'.

'You remind me of two prize fighters circling around one another, not yet ready for the clinch.'

'Philip wants to marry me again.'

'I know.'

Jessica gave her mother an astonished look. 'You knew?'

Dagmar wiped an invisible speck of dust off her camel wool slacks. 'Philip came down to Florida to talk to Ben and myself.'

'When?'

'About a year ago.'

Jessica's astonishment had given way to outrage. 'You mean that Philip talked to you about marrying me again and you didn't *tell* me?'

'Jess, he asked us not to say anything.'

'But didn't you think I should *know*?'

'He talked to us about the divorce and merely said

that sometime in the future he would be getting in touch with you. He didn't know how you'd react, but he didn't want us to think that . . . well, I guess the best way to put it—that his intentions were dishonourable.'

'How could you trust him after the things he did?" Jessica cried.

'What precisely did he do?' Dagmar asked.

'You know how he treated me; you know how cold he was!'

'Jess,' her mother's voice was placating, 'you weren't perfect either.'

Jessica clenched her hands together. 'And what about the baby?'

'What about it?'

'He didn't want it.'

Dagmar shook her head. 'I don't believe that.'

The words came out of Jessica's mouth before she could stop them. 'It was his fault.'

'It was nature's fault, Jess. The baby would have been deformed.'

Tears pricked behind Jessica's eyes. 'You don't know what he said to me.'

'Honey, words don't cause miscarriages.'

No, they didn't and Jessica knew that very well, at least on an intellectual level, but emotionally she felt something far different. She would have liked to tell Dagmar what had actually happened, but whenever she thought of it her throat felt tight as if the memories had gathered there to block the words. Airing the truth would be like opening a Pandora's box of evils; her anger unleashed and free to roam with all its earlier destructive force. Jessica had vivid remembrances of the moment she had torn their wedding photographs to shreds and the day she had ripped apart the necklace Philip had given her for their first anniversary, the pearls scattering throughout the apartment as she threw them in every direction, not caring how priceless they were or how their iridescent surfaces had gleamed at her throat. Jessica hated to remember the day Philip had learned about the baby. She felt the same pain she had felt during the miscarriage—as if a large and impersonal hand were twisting her on the inside, its force cruel, oblivious and inexorable . . .

CHAPTER SEVEN

THE day had dawned like all the others since Jessica had found out that she was pregnant. She woke hugging the secret to her like a child with a precious new toy. It was like owning a rainbow, her own personal gleaming arch into the future, but instead of a pot of gold at the end, there was a baby, a small cuddly baby that she envisioned with Philip's dark hair and her own brown eyes. She saw it lying in a wicker basket strung with pastel ribbons or in a playpen surrounded by colourful toys. She saw it being held in her arms or in Philip's lean hands. She saw the two of them smiling together when the baby discovered its own minute toes or learned to pull itself upright on fat, pudgy legs or spoke its first hesitant word.

Jessica turned on to her back and ran her hands over her breasts and the small curve of her abdomen. There wasn't much evidence of pregnancy yet but her breasts were fuller, their nipples darker and she thought she could detect the slightest swelling of her stomach. She was only seven weeks pregnant, four of which had been spent in ignorance of her state, one in awful contemplation of the possibility and the last two with a slowly growing delight at what a baby would mean to her marriage.

She saw her problems vanishing once Philip knew that he would be a father. To begin with, they'd have to be more settled. A child was a responsibility, and it would need a room and all the paraphernalia of babyhood; a crib, a changing table, a high chair, toys, a tricycle. That meant really considering the apartment as their home instead of a way station. That meant furnishing it at last, getting a carpet for the bedroom and two more chairs for the living room. That meant buying paintings to hang on the bare walls and building bookshelves to house the books that remained unpacked in boxes in their storage space in the basement. Visions of shopping sprees ran through Jessica's head; warm and wonderful afternoons with Philip going from store to store and buying things together.

Then there was his career. Racing was dangerous, and she'd always hated it, knowing how the tension made her insides twist before a race and how fear had ultimately forced her to remain in Manhattan when Philip went away. She could no longer stand the waiting and then the watching, never knowing if this would be the race that would end his life. Jessica was sure that Philip would agree to stop once he became a father. He wouldn't want his son or daughter to grow up without him, and she knew that he'd have no problem finding another career. He was already starting to earn money from endorsements and his business contacts were widespread.

The future looked rosy and Jessica couldn't help smiling to herself as she threw back the covers from the double bed and glanced at the empty side where Philip usually slept. He'd been gone for three weeks, testing another car, and she was expecting him back that evening. She had already spent days planning his return and how she would break the news to him. There would be a candlelit dinner, she would wear a new outfit that she'd bought—a cream silk blouse so low-cut that she couldn't wear a bra and a long, chocolate brown velvet skirt—and then when they were sipping the chilled white wine, the golden flames of the candles flickering between them and music playing softly on the stereo, Jessica would tell him.

She could never quite see beyond this moment or imagine Philip's precise reaction, but how could it be anything other than sheer delight? They'd been married almost four years and, although Philip had often said that he didn't want children, when he was presented with a *fait accompli* Jessica was sure that he'd see it from her point of view. She stood up and stretched, her arms reaching for the ceiling, her balance precariously held on her bare toes. The morning sun streamed in through the window and warmed her shoulder and side through the cotton of her nightgown. It was a good omen, she decided, an augury of a lovely day ahead. Nothing could go wrong when the sky was so blue and she felt so good. Nothing.

'I think I met the man I want to marry,' Megan was saying as they huddled over a table in a crowded deli in the garment district.

'And I think that I've heard that before,' Jessica said as she laced into an onion bagel filled with cream cheese and salmon. She'd hardly suffered from morning sickness and her appetite was healthy and verged on ravenous. When the doctor had told her that she was too thin and should remember that she was eating for two, Jessica had thrown all dietary cautions to the wind.

'This time it's for real,' Megan insisted.

'Uh-uh.'

'No, *honestly*.'

Jessica gave her an exasperated look and then moved over as a waiter squeezed beside their table as he waited on a couple next to them. The restaurant was one of those New York phenomena; a dining place with absolutely no atmosphere or elegance that was jammed at every meal. The tables were a grey formica, the chairs had plastic seats and the walls were strictly utilitarian: they held up the ceiling. But the menu was extensive and the food was superb. Megan and Jessica often met for lunch there; it wasn't far from the apartment and Megan was working for a sweater designer who had offices nearby.

'Okay, I'm all ears.'

Megan put down the pickle she was just about to eat and leaned over the table so that the customers next to them couldn't hear her. 'Rob's collie ran him over in Central Park.'

'Charming.'

'It was love at first sight.'

'I didn't know Rob's collie went in for that sort of thing.'

'Jess! Listen, his name is Simon and he's six foot three and he has a lazy smile that makes my nerve endings twitch and . . .'

'And when are you going to see him again?'

Megan tucked her thick blonde curls behind her ears. 'Next Sunday.'

'Another accidental meeting?'

'He told me that he always jogs in Central Park on Sunday mornings and . . . well, I plan to be there again.'

'With or without the collie?'

'With, of course. I need an excuse, don't you think?'

Jessica gave Megan a loving smile. 'Not that I've usually noticed.'

Megan gave her a return grin. 'You're so easy to talk to,' she said with a note of happy sarcasm. 'I wonder why that is.'

'Longevity and an intimate knowledge of the evil workings of your peculiar little mind.'

'Do you think Simon has a chance?'

Jessica shook her head. 'Nope.'

'Want to make any bets?'

'Six months.'

Megan wrinkled her nose. 'Four on the outside.'

'Five.'

'Okay, you're on. What do you want to bet?'

Jessica took another bite of her bagel and chewed ruminatively. 'You win, I treat you to dinner. I win and you design a wardrobe.'

Megan's blue eyes widened. 'An entire wardrobe. That's pretty stiff.'

'It's not for me.'

'Philip doesn't strike me as the clothes type.'

'It's not for Philip either.' Jessica paused and then sat back, clasping her hands together in sheer joy. 'I've been dying to tell you.'

Megan glanced at Jessica's happy smile and and then down at the half-finished bagel, the salad with creamy cheese dressing, the vanilla milkshake and put two and two together. 'A baby wardrobe?' she asked in disbelief.

Jessica laughed outright. 'Isn't it wonderful?'

'How long have you know?'

'About a month. I'm seven weeks and the baby's due around Christmas and the doctor says that I'm as healthy as a horse and . . .'

'And what does Philip say?'

Jessica's voice sunk to a whisper. 'He doesn't know yet.'

'You haven't told him?' Megan asked in surprise.

'Tonight when he comes back. Oh, Meg, don't you think he's going to be pleased?'

Megan opened her mouth to speak and then closed it as if thinking better of what she was going to say. She picked up a spoon and swirled it in her coffee for a few seconds and then spoke, 'I thought you and Philip had been fighting a lot recently.'

Jessica brushed Megan's words aside with a quick flick of her wrist. 'That's going to be over now.'

'I thought you said that Philip wasn't keen on having kids.'

'When he has one, he'll love it.' Jessica's voice held happy conviction.

'Jess.' Megan looked up from an intent mixing of her coffee. 'I'm not sure that Philip is going to be quite as ecstatic as . . .'

Jessica leaned forward. 'Don't you see, Meg? It's going to change everything between us for the better. We've been arguing over such trivial things, but none of that's important now that there'll be a baby to think about. We'll need furniture and baby stuff, maybe we'll even have to get another apartment. The one we've got now is a bit small even though it does have two bedrooms. I've thought about a house but I don't think that either Philip or I are suburban types, do you? And . . .' She talked on and on, her brown eyes wide and happy, her hands making expressive pictures in the air, her face bright with anticipation, never noticing that Megan had stopped speaking and was unable to meet her eyes. Jessica was far too engrossed in her own dreams for that.

The table in the dining room was perfect even though it was old and a crack ran down its centre. Jessica had covered it with white linen and set it with the china, silver and stemware her parents had given her at her marriage; elegant white bone china with a garland of vines on the border, carved silver and delicate goblets with silvered rims. The candles were a pale green to match the leaves on the plates, and she'd bought a small centrepiece of flowers; pale yellow roses set against fine-edged ferns. The table sat in a small nook off the galley kitchen, and it was the one spot in the apartment that was actually cosy. All the other rooms were too large and too bare for the meagre amount of furniture that Jessica and Philip owned.

Jessica wore the silk blouse with its bow that tied just in the valley between her breasts and her long skirt swept against the straps of her high-heeled beige sandals. She wore her hair down as Philip liked it, pulled back from her temples with silver combs, its black length cascading down her back. She felt sophisticated, beautiful and sexy—not 'motherly' at all, but then that wasn't how she wanted Philip to see her. Without quite admitting it to herself, Jessica had pinned an extraordinary number of hopes and wishes on the baby she carried within her. She wanted it to cement a marriage that seemed to be hopelessly heading towards destruction; she dreamed of it as a new source of tenderness and of affection; and even deeper in her heart, she desperately hoped that the pregnancy and baby would cause Philip to see her in a new light—as a woman in the fullest sense of the word; mature, sensual and feminine.

She hummed to herself as she chose a stack of records for the stereo and began to take the discs out of their covers; a bit of jazz, a touch of classical and some movie tracks to set the mood. She didn't want the music to interfere with their conversation; she just wanted it to be a pleasant complement. It was important that she and Philip mend their fences before she would be able to tell him about the baby; they hadn't parted on the best of terms and he'd only phoned her once while he was gone.

A frown passed over her face when she thought about his leaving. She had, of course, not wanted him to go. She hated his constant trips and she'd begun to hate his cars. Philip lavished upon them a singular care and affection and in her mind Jessica saw them as enemies; steel and leather enemies with a seductive appeal that she couldn't match no matter how hard she tried. Sometimes, she even had the bitter thought that she would have preferred it if Philip ran around with other women—at least she could compete in that arena, instead of fighting a useless and ultimately losing battle against machinery.

But she'd never been able to articulate her feelings to Philip; he would have laughed at her, so Jessica took out her frustrations in other ways. On the day that Philip had left, she had initiated an argument; a needling, designed-to-irritate argument and she'd been highly successful. Philip had marched out of the apartment without a goodbye kiss or even an embrace, his mouth tight with anger. She'd been haughty when he left but the façade only lasted until the door slammed behind him. Then she'd collapsed on the couch and cried, her face buried in her hands, wondering why she had even mentioned the shelf she wanted him to build in the kitchen, knowing that if she nagged him again that she'd make him furious. She wasn't introspective enough to understand that, for her, the shelf had merely been another way of testing Philip's affections. If he loved her, he'd build it—if he didn't, then he obviously didn't care.

But three weeks had given her time to reflect, her pregnancy had been confirmed and she wasn't a pessimist by nature. Jessica had finally brushed aside memories of the argument and concentrated on all the wonderful things that a child would bring to her. Anticipation had conjured up the candlelit meal, the elegant and sexy outfit and the soft music. Anticipation made her mouth twitch upwards at the ends. And anticipation made her move quickly around the apartment, straightening a pillow on the couch, a napkin on the table, giving the final touches to what she saw as the beginning of a marvellous evening.

The click of the lock made her whirl around, her heart starting to beat furiously, and she rushed to the door, opening it just as Philip was reaching down to pick up his suitcase. She stood there, a welcoming smile on her face, as he slowly straightened up, his silvery eyes running the length of her slim body and then coming to rest on her shining eyes.

'Are you going somewhere?' he asked.

'No, I just . . .'

He walked past her into the apartment, his arm brushing against her shoulder, a tall figure in beige jacket and jeans, his dark hair ruffled on his forehead. Jessica closed the door behind him and stood with her back to it as Philip surveyed the apartment, his gaze coming to rest on the dining room table with its gleaming goblets and china, their surfaces reflecting the leaping flames of the candles.

He put down his suitcase and began to unzip his

jacket. 'Were you entertaining someone?' he asked with cold politeness.

Jessica was hurt but then she reminded herself that he didn't know about the baby, that he hadn't had three weeks to think about their wonderful future. 'No,' she said. 'This is for you.'

He gave her a quick glance. 'Is it?'

'Of course,' she said, walking up to him and resting her fingertips on the sleeve of his dark shirt. 'This is a welcoming dinner. You've been gone a long time.'

His eyes were wary as they looked down at the slender oval of her face. 'What are you up to, Jess?'

'Nothing,' she insisted.

'If you're still angling for that damned shelf,' he growled, 'then you can forget it.'

'I'm not,' she protested. 'I don't care about the shelf. It isn't important.'

A tension seemed to abate within him and he ran a weary hand through his hair, ruffling it even further. Jessica stood up on her tiptoes and kissed him lightly on the lips. 'I'm glad you're home,' she said.

He pulled her up to him, his kiss hard and thorough, making Jessica's legs feel weak and causing a rush of familiar warmth to her groin. Three weeks had been a long time to sleep alone, and she felt the hunger welling up inside of her, a sensual craving that made her begin to unbutton Philip's shirt so that she could run her hands down the length of his chest, feeling the hard planes of his muscles and the beat of his heart beneath her fingertips. But the minute he felt her fingers on his bare skin, Philip pushed her away and held her at arm's length, his eyes narrowing.

'You want something,' he said flatly.

Jessica looked wounded. 'No.'

'Come on. You always want something.'

'Why do you have such a mercenary mind?' she asked angrily. 'Why can't I have a generous impulse and act on it?'

'Because, my sweet charmer, it is such a rare occurrence.'

Jessica fought to keep the tears away. 'You enjoy hurting me, don't you?'

Philip shrugged as he picked up his suitcase and headed into the bedroom. 'It was just a comment,' he said. 'Don't take it so personally.'

Jessica watched his tall figure go through the bedroom door and she unwillingly followed him. She would have liked to leave the apartment, to storm out in a rage, but there was the baby to think about and she was determined to make the evening go right despite its disastrous start. She watched him place the suitcase on the bed and throw it open. 'Did you have a good time?' she asked.

Philip gave her a curious glance as he took out a folded pile of shirts. 'It was okay,' he replied laconically and she knew that he wasn't going to volunteer any more information. It was a typical exchange; she was cautious about probing into his professional life and he resisted any effort she made to find out what he was doing. Jessica had often felt as if his career stood between them like a wall of granite.

'Brad phoned while you were gone.' Brad was Philip's accountant.

'What did he want?'

'I don't know. He wants to see you.'

'Fine.' He pulled out a suit and hung it in the closet.

'My parents phoned.'

'And?' he asked from the depths of the closet.

'They'll be coming to New York next week. My father has some business here in the city.' It was a visit Jessica was looking forward to—she hadn't yet told her parents that they could look forward to a grandchild.

His face was in profile to her, its outline harsh. 'That should make you happy,' he said sarcastically.

Jessica stared at him for a minute and then, the baby all but forgotten, she clenched her hands into tight fists.

'Why do you say that?' she asked, her voice a challenge. She felt the fight coming; it was inevitable and she no longer cared whether the evening was serene and joyous. For several months, Philip had been making snide remarks about her parents and she was damned if she was going to let him get away with it again.

Philip gave her a cold look. 'Why? Because you're still attached to them, sweetheart. I know you call your father everytime we have a fight.'

She gritted her teeth. 'I don't.'

'The phone bill doesn't lie.'

'I don't discuss our private life with them.'

'How kind of you,' he drawled.

She could feel the blood rushing to her face as anger swept through her. Philip always had this effect on her. Their fights began with innuendo, grew into insults and then developed into an all-out brawl with Philip getting cooler by the minute as Jessica became filled with rage.

'I would like to know what you've got against my family,' she demanded.

'It's not them, darling, it's the umbilical cord that stretches between New York and Washington. All you have to do is tug a bit and they come running.'

'They love me. Is there anything wrong with that?'

'They treat you as if you were five instead of twenty-five.'

'The trouble with you, Philip, is that you haven't the faintest notion of what parental love is all about.'

He snapped the suitcase shut and lifted it off the bed. 'I think you'd benefit from some probing of your own psyche,' he replied icily, 'instead of spending all your time delving into mine.'

The blood had rushed into Jessica's cheeks. 'Now you're going to tell me that everything is *my* fault.'

Philip finally looked at her directly, one dark eyebrow raised in a mocking arch. 'Why are women so vague?' he asked. 'What precisely is "everything".'

'Our marriage, the fighting, this goddamned empty

apartment.' Jessica didn't care what she was saying anymore. She only knew that a venom was rising within her, a black hatred that came out in poisoned, barbed words.

'What's wrong with the apartment?' Philip looked around at the bedroom with its spartan furnishings; the double bed covered with a pale blue spread, two dressers and one night table with a squat blue lamp with a white shade. The window had curtains; Philip had refused to buy any so Jessica had sewn them. Unfortunately, she'd never learned to be a seamstress so the draperies were a plain white cotton with a slightly uneven hem.

'What's wrong with it?' she echoed shrilly. 'Everything—it's ugly, it isn't a home, it looks like a motel.'

'I told you—I'm not the type to settle down. You knew that when we got married.'

'But I don't have to like it,' she hissed.

Philip gave one of his infuriating shrugs as he heaved the suitcase on to the upper shelf of his closet. 'Tough, sweetheart.'

Jessica felt her heart beating with heavy, awkward-feeling thumps. It was the way her heart felt when she was nervous or frightened, when she knew that something awful was about to occur. She steeled herself to ask the question, the inevitable, terrifying question. 'You really don't care about me, do you?'

Philip turned to her, the silvery eyes cold and metallic. 'Not the way your parents do.'

'That isn't what I asked.'

'But that's what you really want, isn't it?'

'No, I . . .'

'Face it, Jess. You don't want love from me—you want to be pampered, soothed, gratified and humoured. You were born with a silver spoon in your mouth and you've never quite got rid of the feeling that you deserve more than the world wants to give you.' He walked past her back into the living room where he sat down on the couch and picked up a newspaper, his long blue-jeaned legs stretched out before him, his booted feet crossed at the ankles.

Jessica was shaking with fury, her hands trembling with the effort to keep from hitting out, from slapping him across the face, from slashing at him with her fingernails. She wanted to hurt him the way he had hurt her; she wanted to lacerate his ego; she wanted to tear a strip off his cool and hateful façade. She marched out after him and stood before him, her hands on her hips, her chin held high.

'You're a selfish egotist,' she threw at him.

Philip slowly put down the newspaper. 'You don't want to give up, do you?'

'Nothing matters to you except your cars.'

The newspaper was tossed aside with an angry flourish. 'Damn it, Jess. What the hell do you want from me?'

'Some consideration, some affection, some *husbandly*,' she almost sneered as she said the word, 'devotion.'

'You don't want a husband; you want a doting father,' he said, grinding the words out between his teeth.

'That's not true,' she yelled, feeling the lump starting to form in her throat and the tears prick behind her eyes. Why couldn't Philip be softer and more gentle? Why couldn't he understand that all she wanted was his love? Why did he have to be harsh and callous?

'You're damn right, it's true,' he said, standing up and striding towards the window that overlooked another building and a busy street below. He looked down at the rushing cars below, his expression dark and moody. 'You're a baby, Jess. A whining, clingy child who needs constant affection and support. That shelf, for instance. If you're so set on it, why don't you put it up yourself? This is the era of women's liberation, remember? You know what a hammer looks like.'

'I . . . I thought we'd do it together.'

'Together—it's one of your favourite words. You want to do everything together. You'd fill my time with things you want to do. It's damn suffocating, if you want to know the truth.'

She stamped her foot in utter frustration. 'We're married. We're supposed to do things together.'

'You don't give me any space. I can't breathe, damn it!'

The tears welled in her eyes; tears of anger, of frustration and of self-pity. 'Why did you marry me?' she whispered.

A muscle clenched in his jaw. 'I don't know sometimes.'

'It . . . was sex, wasn't it?'

'Most men marry for sex.'

She was sinking down to the floor, her knees crumpling, her hands up before her face so that he wouldn't see the tears crumpling, her hands up before her face so that he wouldn't see the tears slipping down her cheeks. The long brown skirt billowed around her; her head bent forward so that her thick dark hair fell on each side of her cheeks. In a funny sort of way, Jessica felt like she was two people; the woman on the floor who felt as if a knife had been turned within her and a cold, outside observer who was watching the woman on the floor, knowing the picture that she made and despising her for being so pitiful, so begging and so helpless.

'For god's sake, Jess. Stop being so dramatic. You knew the truth.'

She shook her head. 'I didn't,' she said, her voice low and shaky.

'It was the same for you.'

'No.'

'Except that women like to cover up their sexual urges with romantic illusions.'

His voice was so cold that Jessica shivered. 'No,' she whispered.

Philip made a sound of disgust and walked towards a chair. Jessica looked up at him, her face streaked with tears, her mouth trembling. 'Where are you going?' she asked as he picked up his jacket.

'Out.'

'But I made dinner.'

Philip looked over at the table with its fluttering candles and pretty place settings. 'I'm not hungry.' He pulled the jacket on and, zipping it up, walked towards the door.

'Philip . . .' Jessica's voice was full of entreaty.

'Don't wait up.'

'Philip, I'm . . . pregnant.'

He stopped dead before the door, his back suddenly rigid. 'What?'

'I'm pregnant.'

He turned around slowly. 'Whose is it?'

'My god,' she cried, 'it's yours!'

Her voice held too much conviction for Philip to disbelieve her. His lips set in a straight, hard line and deep grooves ran from his nose to his mouth. 'When?' he asked.

'The . . . night we went to dinner with the Jamisons.'

'I thought you were using birth control.'

'I forgot . . . I didn't expect . . .' Her voice trailed off.

He looked at her for a second and then said, 'That was two months ago.'

'The doctor said I was fine and the baby is . . .'

'You wouldn't have any trouble getting an abortion.'

Abortion. The word hung in the sudden silence as Jessica stared at Philip, her eyes wide in horror. Abortion. He wanted her to get rid of the baby, to have it torn out of her body like so much useless detritus, leaving her empty and barren, her dreams smashed and broken. Abortion . . .

'I'm sure your doctor . . .'

'Never.' The word came out flat and cold and determined.

Philip ignored her. 'It's not too late . . .'

'*Never.*' Jessica stood up; her knees no longer trembled, her eyes were dry and her hands were steady although they felt as cold as ice.

Philip took a step forward. 'Don't be a crazy fool,' he said. 'We don't want a child.'

'You don't,' she said pointedly. 'I do.'

'You're not mature enough to have a child.'

'Then it must be that I'm not mature enough to be your wife.' There—the words were out, spoken, vibrating between them, their meaning implicit and obvious.

'Are you giving me an ultimatum?' Philip asked harshly.

'You can call it anything you please.' Jessica was surprisingly calm now that the issue was out in the open. There would be no more theatrical, teary moments, no more supplication on her side and dominance on his, no more pointless, useless fights.

Philip was silent and their eyes met. Jessica stood firm beneath that glittering gaze, a slender figure in a crumpled velvet skirt with tear-stained cheeks. She'd bitten her lipstick off and the skin around her eyes was darkened by mascara, but she had no interest in what she looked like. She no longer cared if Philip saw her as desirable and feminine. In fact, she'd just come to the conclusion that she no longer cared what Philip thought of her at all.

'Are you,' he asked in a low voice, 'asking for a divorce?'

This time she was the one to give a nonchalant shrug. 'I'm going to have the baby,' she said, 'with you or without you.'

His shoulder muscles bunched beneath the fabric of his jacket. 'Jess, you're acting like a fool. Our marriage won't stand a baby; it can barely stand on its own as it is.'

'I don't care.'

'What are you trying to do? Force me into a separation?' If Jessica hadn't known differently, she might have thought that Philip sounded desperate and unhappy, but he'd made it painfully clear over the years that he didn't suffer from the emotional states of ordinary people—the only feelings Philip was capable of were exasperation, irritation and anger.

'You'll have to make a choice, I guess.' Her tone was careless.

'Why?' he grated. 'Why do you have to have this baby?'

Jessica paused for a second. It was an odd question, not one that she had expected and she wasn't quite sure how to answer it. Originally she had wanted the baby only for what she thought would be its beneficial effect on her marriage, but Philip's reaction had brought home to her how unrealistic she had been. The baby was no panacea; it had no magical powers that could make her marital problems disappear into thin air. It was a person, an individual in its own right, and she had suddenly grown fiercely protective of the life that lay within her, this child she had conceived in a moment of careless love-making. It was hers and it had a right to live no matter that Philip, its own father, wished to deny its existence.

'Because it's my child,' she said simply.

In two strides, Philip was before her, grabbing her by the shoulders and shaking her so hard that her head wobbled back and forth. 'It's mine, too and I don't want it!'

'I'm sorry.'

'Damn it, Jess! Don't you see that this is the end?'

'If that's how you feel . . .'

The silver eyes glared down at her. 'You're pushing me!' She shook her head helplessly. 'A child . . . would be impossible!'

'I'm leaving you,' she said, and the next words followed with a deadly logic and precision. 'I don't want to be married to you anymore.'

Philip dropped his hands from her shoulders and his mouth slanted in a bitter, twisted line. 'And I,' he said, his voice low and cold and sinister, 'wouldn't want to be married to you if you were the last woman on earth.' He turned on his heel and walked out the door, slamming it behind him with such force that the candles flickered on the table and one goblet fell over, its rim shattering against the edge of a plate.

Jessica turned to look at the table with its shimmering candlelight and pale green napkins set in their silver holders. She had arranged the whole evening with such innocence, polishing the silver and goblets to a bright sheen, polishing her hopes until they glittered like jewels. Now, it was all over, the anticipation dead, her hopes dulled beyond recognition, the jewels revealed as false—all paste and glass and illusion. If she hadn't been so blind, so willingly obtuse, she would have known all along that nothing, not even a baby, could have saved her marriage, and it struck Jessica with heavy irony that her relationship with Philip had become so barren at the same time that her body had quickened with their child.

She walked over to the table and began to pile up the plates. She wasn't crying; she felt numb as if shock had anaesthetized her feelings. In an almost mindless fashion, she replaced the knives, spoons and forks in the silver chest and refolded the napkins. The goblets went back on to their shelf in the narrow kitchen and the candles, their wicks black and curled, went into a drawer. Jessica thought of nothing as her hands moved through the motions. She would only later see the *un*setting of that table as symbolic; each plate, each spoon, each glass representing the bits and pieces of her marriage as they were put to a final rest.

It wasn't until she was finished and the table was bare once again that Jessica felt the first pain. It was a sharp streak in her lower back and she straightened up, her hand instinctively pressing against the muscle, thinking that she must have hurt herself bending to put the tablecloth away. But the pain returned, keener and more distinct, low and to one side. It came in spasms, making her suck in her breath at its strength, her hands clenching until her nails cut into her palms. She tried everything; aspirin, hot packs, lying down in a curled-up position, lying on her front, lying on her back. Not until midnight was Jessica able to face what was happening, and it was then that the dark anger began, born from that primitive side of her that believed, despite all her intellectual reasoning, that Philip had killed their child just as surely as if he had twisted a knife himself.

CHAPTER EIGHT

THE nightmares began on the third night after Ben and Dagmar had returned to Florida and after a day of gardening when Jessica had worked herself into exhaustion, seeking relief from her thoughts and hoping that physical fatigue would help her to sleep better. It had come to her as a shock that Philip's accident had not been the catalyst that had convinced him to marry her again. He had planned his re-entry into her life; he had been thinking about it for at least a year. He'd even had the audacity to approach her parents and win them over to his side before taking his first step in her direction. Jessica had found it easy to dismiss Philip's intentions as convalescent desires, but she couldn't shrug off the knowledge that his return was part of a long-term strategy. She wondered if his present I-am-a-pleasant-roommate façade would last much longer; and she was apprehensive that he would make some devastating move. She was already too aware of him, sensitised to his presence to the point that she knew whenever and wherever he was in the house as if she had developed antennae. She was on the constant edge of tension and it made her wary, uneasy and susceptible to insomnia.

But she'd gone to bed that night with the heavenly feeling that she was going to sleep like a log at long last. Her muscles ached with that pleasant agony that comes of hard labour, her nose was sunburned from long hours outside and her mind felt quiet and at peace. She dropped off almost instantaneously after turning out the lights, and when the screams began she was sleeping so solidly that, at first, she thought they were issuing from her own mouth.

The screams were hoarse and masculine, filling the upper storey of the house and coming right through the wall to her bedroom. Jessica was on her feet and running within seconds, arriving at Philip's room just as the night table lamp was switched on. She threw open the door and stood there for a second, blinking at the sudden effect of the light on her eyes.

When she could finally focus, she saw Philip lying across the bed with his forearm across his eyes, the arc of lamplight encircling his head in a mock halo. The covers were twisted across and around him, the bedspread was jammed into a corner of the headboard and a pillow had been thrown on to the floor. The room looked as if Philip had wrestled with some monumental, occult force and lost. He seemed helpless and vulnerable, bare from the waist up, a sheet wrapped around his hips, one pyjamaed leg hanging over the edge of the bed.

Jessica walked uncertainly to the edge of the bed. 'Are you all right?' she asked in concern.

Philip moved his arm down and she was shocked to see the dark circles under his eyes and the grey pallor of his skin. 'It was the dream,' he said wearily. 'The damn dream. It keeps coming back.'

'You mean you've had it before? I've never heard . . .'

'I've always been able to stop it,' he said, 'but this time I couldn't.'

'What kind of a dream?' she asked softly.

He took a deep breath and sat up slightly, his head dark against the white case of a pillow. 'I've had it many times. I'm running through blank space, either heading towards death or having it on my heels. Someone is trying to kill me and I can't seem to decide whether I want the confrontation or I'm running away from it.'

'Who . . .?'

He shrugged unhappily. 'Who knows? Death could be anything—a monster, a man without a face, a veiled woman—I've dreamt every cliché in the book.'

She shivered. 'It's frightening.'

'Yes,' he acknowledged, leaning his head back against the pillow and closing his eyes in utter fatigue. It came to Jessica as she watched him that Philip had changed immensely. He was almost thirty-five and no longer had that restless virility of a young man. He was older, more mature, his masculinity underscored by a new depth of emotion and feeling. The Philip of seven years ago would never have admitted to her that he had terrifying dreams; he would have suppressed them, hidden his vulnerabilities in the dark curve of the night.

'Will you be okay now?' she asked.

He nodded, his eyes still closed. 'It usually doesn't come back for a few weeks.'

But the dream came back the next night and then the night after that. Philip woke in the mornings looking as if he hadn't slept and, for the first time, Jessica noticed silver hairs at his temples. He dragged himself to his physiotherapy sessions and not even a new cast, a shorter walking one with a heel built in that not only gave him more mobility but also allowed him the use of his knee, cheered him up. Jessica would find him sitting on the porch, staring into the trees that bordered the backyard, a book unopened on his lap. They didn't talk about the nights; there seemed to be a mutual and non-spoken agreement between them that Philip had to fight his own demons as best he could. Jessica would lie in bed listening to the sounds coming through her wall and wait until they were over, usually in a matter of seconds. Sometimes there would be silence after that or she would hear Philip get up and go down the stairs. Sometimes, she had an overpowering urge to go to him, but she was afraid of rejection, his resistance to the comforting she had offered him during their marriage vivid in her memory.

On the fifth night, the screams seemed to go on forever and Jessica could no longer stand the sounds. The master bedroom was unlit when she entered and she could hear Philip thrashing around as he moaned. She had to shake him, her hands on his bare shoulders, her voice urgent in the darkness. 'Philip, wake up!'

'Jess?' he muttered.

'Yes.'

'My god,' he said, his breathing still ragged, his chest rising and falling with the effort.

'Philip, this has to stop. Maybe you should see someone.' She reached for the light, but he restrained her with his hand.

'Hold me for a while,' he begged.

So she lay there beside him, his head resting on the curve of her shoulder, his arms wrapped around her waist. She had one hand on his broad back and the other was against his chest where the dark triangle of hair formed a peak. Their legs met under the sheets; at the thigh, knee and ankle, and it was wonderful, Jessica admitted to herself, to hold Philip like this, to feel his breath against her skin at the open collar of her nightgown and the deep beating of his heart under her palm.

'The same dream?' she asked.

He shuddered. 'I couldn't get out of it.'

'Philip, I think most people have dreams like yours except that're not so repetitive.' Jessica could remember nightmares she'd had; particularly one she'd dreamed as a child where a voracious animal, like a fox or wolf, was preparing to eat her.

'It's from my past.'

'You mean you had it as a child?'

He nodded. 'I told you—I wanted to die as a kid, I wanted to make my parents happy. I don't have to see a psychiatrist to know that the dream is a death wish of sorts.'

'But you're not a child anymore . . .'

'No, but the feeling remains. I sublimated it in racing.'

Suddenly, Jessica felt some of the pieces from her

past fall into place. 'You raced to die?' she asked in a low voice.

'I'd been racing since I was a kid, first bikes and then old cars and finally breaking into the circuit professionally. I've known for a long time, Jess, that part of me wanted to race because I hoped it would kill me.'

Quite unconsciously, Jessica pulled him closer into her arms and pressed her cheek against the top of his head, feeling his flesh beneath her hands and his breath moving against her skin. A nausea rose in her at the thought of his vibrancy, his very aliveness, housing a desire for death. She began to understand his grim humour and the way he had held himself aloof before every race. He had faced black shadows every time he pulled the racing helmet over his head and climbed into his car.

'I wanted death but I flirted with it,' he went on. 'Part of me believed that I was invincible; death couldn't catch me the way it did the others. I was too strong and too smart for that.' He gave a low, self-deprecating laugh. 'I was such a damned fool.'

'I thought you loved racing.'

'That's the paradox of it. I did; I was defying death, conquering it with every race even if I didn't win. I grew more and more reckless as the years went by until I finally made a mistake. It was my fault that I crashed—it was an error in judgment, a step on the accelerator instead of the brake. I'm just lucky that I'm alive at all.'

'I hated it,' she said quietly.

His arms tightened around her. 'I know you did, but death was so seductive, Jess. I can't explain how it felt to start a race with the adrenalin flowing and every sense alive, waiting for the ambush, the moment when death would stare you in the face and you could laugh back at it, sneer at it, prove once again that you were a man.' He paused for a second and then went on, 'I couldn't give up racing when we were married. It was the only way I knew that I existed.'

'But you existed for me!'

'No, you thought I was someone else, a man of your own imagining. You didn't have a clue who I was.'

Jessica was silent for a moment, absorbing his words and knowing they were true. She'd been far too young and far too self-absorbed to have any idea of what lay behind Philip's façade. She hadn't understood enough about human nature to make the connection between his unhappy childhood and the man he had grown to be. It had only been recently, since she'd started writing, that Jessica had realised that no person stands isolated from the past.

'That's why you were so cold to me,' she finally said.

He pulled himself up so that their faces were close. 'I was afraid of loving you too much, Jess. Afraid that it would make me frightened to take chances. That's what it takes to be a top driver: skill and a willingness to push that skill beyond its limit.' He touched her face tenderly with his hand as if he could read her expression through his fingertips. 'Jess, I'm sorry for the way I treated you. I should never have married you, but I couldn't help myself. I loved you too much.'

Jessica sat silently as he caressed her cheeks, her temples and then the flowing length of her hair. Emotions welled up in her, fountain of feelings, complex and overwhelming. Tears formed in her eyes, at their corners and slipped to her temples.

'Jess! Jess, don't cry!' Philip touched his mouth to her wet skin, his tongue tasting the salt of her tears.

'You made me so unhappy.'

'I'd do anything if I could only start all over and change what happened. I've cursed myself for what I did, hated myself for making you so miserable. Jess, I love you—I always have.'

'Oh, Philip.' She was crying openly now, sobs tearing at her chest. 'I wanted to hear you say that so badly.'

He was kissing her, his mouth on her forehead, on

her eyes and finally reaching her trembling mouth. His
arms were around her, cradling her against the hardness
of his chest and rocking her slightly, as if she were a child,
as if he could comfort her with that very primitive motion.
'Don't cry,' he whispered. 'Hush.'

'We wasted all those years,' she said.

'We'll make them up.'

'We can't,' she sobbed.

'Yes, we can,' he said urgently. 'We'll get married and
start again.'

'I don't know . . . I'm not sure . . . I . . .'

His response was physical; his mouth and tongue
meeting hers, his hand slipping under the hem of her
nightgown to run the length of her naked side, along
the slender line of her leg, the curve of her hip and then
arriving at her breast to cup its fullness. It was such a
natural move, emerging from a moment of emotional
intimacy and caring that Jessica welcomed the feel of
his warm fingers on her skin, her breast swelling into
his palm, her hips rolling to meet his, her mouth fully
responsive beneath his lips. For a second they remained
pressed together, and then Philip slipped his leg between
hers. 'You feel so good,' he murmured and Jessica could
have said the same. She was touching him wherever her
hands reached and revelling in the masculinity of him; the
muscles of his back rippling beneath her fingers, the
hardness of his flesh against her stomach.

He lifted her nightgown higher so that his mouth
could take her breast. His teeth and tongue played with
one sensitive nipple, his breath alternately cooling and
warming its swollen tissues. Jessica arched her back as
all rationality gave way to instinct and thought yielded
to passion. She felt his touching of her breast reach
deep within her to where desire was centred, its heat
radiating out. The years of celibacy washed away as
if they were nothing; her body knew every hint,
every nuance, of love-making. She knew when to
slip her hands beneath the waistband of his pyjamas,

when to move her fingers.

Their motions were so synchronised, so harmonious, so in step with one another, that no words were necessary. She didn't have to say when she wished to be touched; he could sense it by the falling apart of her legs and the slight rise of her hips. She cried out at his intimate caress, that golden stroke of sensuality that penetrated deep inside, and then cried out again when his fingers moved, touched and circled. Her nightgown was pulled over her head and thrown to the floor; his pyjama pants fell on top of it. They were reduced to the most elemental state of all; a man and a woman, naked and entwined in a bed.

He entered her slowly and the filling of her made Jessica's head fall back, her eyes closed in ecstasy, her fingers clenching his shoulders above her. It had been so long, so very long, and she hadn't known until now how much she had hungered for satiation. That hunger drove her to move against him in a slowly increasing pace, the rhythmic thrusting ever stronger and deeper. Moving, joining, meeting; Philip's mouth was still on hers, his hands gripping the strong muscles of her buttocks. 'Please . . .' she whispered at last and one hand slid between their bodies, touching her intimately as they moved and Jessica spiralled towards the final peak of sensation, hovering at its edge and then tumbling over, downward into the release of warm, dark velvet contractions. Above her, Philip trembled and then arched, his arm hard around her as if he wanted her all, and then he collapsed over her, their bodies slick from love, their hearts beating in rapid unison.

Jessica woke the following morning when a crow outside the window called to its mate and she opened her eyes to find that she was facing Philip. They were curled on opposite sides, their knees touching, his hand lightly circling her wrist. He was sleeping peacefully, the hard planes of his face relaxed, his dark hair tousled on the pillow. Jessica lay there, wanting to wake him but also knowing how badly he needed rest. She wanted to place her hand along the curve of his cheek and watch his eyes open, their depths silvery and mysterious. She wanted to see his gathering recognition, his remembering and his slow and sensual smile. She longed to have him place his arm around her and pull her into the warm curve of his body, but she lay still, unwilling to disturb his peace. The long wakeful nights had taken their toll of his energy and his sleep was healing and restorative. Jessica moved cautiously, slipping out from under the covers and picking her nightgown up off the floor before leaving the room. He muttered in his sleep as she went, but his eyes remained closed and he was soon breathing deeply again as she closed the door silently behind her.

She showered, letting the hot spray of water beat on her skin where every nerve ending held a lingering sensation of pleasure. She wanted to raise her arms to the sky and embrace the sun so great was the sudden vitality that she had, the intoxicating sense that she'd been liberated into extraordinary freedom. She hadn't ever meant to sleep with Philip again, but her body had been urgent, its need for satisfaction overwhelming. Celibacy, she was discovering, had been a cage, a cell and a prison for her emotions, forcing her to lead a life of harsh loneliness and an existence of denial and restraint. Jessica hadn't the slightest clue if she wanted to marry Philip and she didn't care about the ramifications of being his lover. She only wished to savour the moment, explore the new terrain of her sensuality and rediscover the depths of her passion. Philip had pulled away the heavy, dark shroud of her self-imposed isolation and, for the first time in years, Jessica felt like a woman again—her femininity released, the wellspring of her sexuality tapped, its force restored to flow and surge once again.

And the energy that was released in her had another effect on Jessica, one that she would never have foreseen or expected. As she stepped out of the shower and pulled a towel off the rack, wrapping it around her, she suddenly realised that she wanted to write again. She stopped for a second and stared at her image in the foggy mirror where her face was a white blur, her eyes smudges of dark brown. The thought of her career floundering and breaking on a case of writer's block had been so painful to her that Jessica had avoided thinking about her writing at all for weeks.

She seemed to have lost all sense of the skills she had once possessed and in which she had taken great pride. She had, at one time, been a thorough and astute researcher, a probing and yet sympathetic interviewer and a writer who had been able to define the lives of other women for the reader as universal experiences. These were the talents which had got Jessica to the top in a highly competitive field, and it was precisely these talents that had failed her the last time she had tried to put pen to paper. Her research had seemed inadequate, the few interviews she had done with unwed mothers had seemed dull and she couldn't seem to focus on any particular theme. At first she had blamed her writer's block on Philip's arrival in her life, but now she realised that his coming had only aggravated a problem with roots deep in the dour isolation of her life. How could she write about women whose babies represented sexuality in its most unhindered force when she denied her own passions so vehemently?

Philip had done more than reawaken her sensuality and her femininity, Jessica realised. His touch had magically reawakened her desire to work again, and the very thought of it gave her a sense of exhilaration so pervasive she could feel it right down to the tips of her fingers. She hurriedly got dressed, not bothering to put up her hair, grabbed a cup of coffee for breakfast and went to the study where she pulled out all of her research on unwed mothers and, piling it on her desk, began to sort through her notes and filing cards. There was so much material to cover, so many studies, analyses and case histories that she had hours of work before her. Jessica plunged into her papers, all sense of time lost; the only sound in the study that of her pencil as she worked, filling in line after line on the pad of yellow legal paper before her . . .

She had no idea how many hours had gone by until a slight noise made her look up to find Philip standing in the doorway, leaning on his cane, his figure tall and lean in a dark blue velour gown, his hair still tousled from sleep.

'You're writing,' he said.

Jessica nodded, looked down at the paper before her and cleared her throat. The sight of him brought back all the memories of the night before, and the thought of the intimacies they had shared suddenly made her shy of him, the way a young girl might be shy when a man comes to court her. 'I . . . I'm starting the book on unwed mothers,' she stammered, pushing a long strand of black hair out of her eyes. 'I've put it off for a long time.'

'I see.'

'There's a lot to cover.' She waved at the pile of papers and books.

The grey eyes told her nothing. 'Yes.'

'And I still have to do a few more interviews and . . .' Jessica could hear her own voice rattling on and on, bright and cheerful, while her mind took in the details of Philip's face and body; the enigmatic eyes, the unsmiling mouth, the hand jammed into one pocket, the shoulder leaning against the door jamb. '. . . and— oh god, it's late isn't it?'

'Eleven o'clock.'

'I have a lunch with Daniel . . . some contracts to sign . . . have to make a living, you know . . .' Why was she babbling on so idiotically, the smile plastered on her face? Why didn't Philip stop her? Why didn't he just step forward and take her in his arms and stop the nervous beating of her heart?

But he didn't do anything of the kind. He listened to her, shifted his weight slightly, winced a bit when he stepped on his injured foot, and then turned away, saying, 'You sound very busy. I won't keep you.'

Jessica had the urge to fly out of her chair and run after him as he limped away, but shyness and a sudden uncertainty held her to the seat. There had been nothing of the Philip she had known last night in the man standing in her doorway. This Philip was reminiscent of the man she had married; cool and aloof, his thoughts a mystery, the emotions behind the mask unknown and frightening. All the feelings of vulnerability and inadequacy that had plagued Jessica during their marriage now tumbled back upon her, chaining her to her chair and stopping her from taking that opening step towards understanding and reconciliation. And it was humiliating to discover that neither her successes nor her hard-won maturity could quiet fears that she had thought were gone forever. They had remained, it seemed, locked within her like a Pandora's box of unwanted emotions, ready to fly out at the slightest release.

'And the good news is that *All's Fair* has also been picked up by several European magazines for serialisation,' Daniel was saying as they sat opposite one another in the restaurant near his office. It was one of the few dining places in Washington that had a four-star rating and a consistently good reputation for elegantly prepared French food impeccably served in luxurious surroundings—stained glass windows, plush carpeting, and Louis XIV furniture. 'How does it feel to be an international star?'

'Not a star,' she protested.

'An internationally known name, a household name in thirty countries.'

'Like Ajax?' she asked. 'Or Pepsodent?'

Daniel waved a scolding finger at her. 'You've no sense of dignity,' he chided, but his eyes were admiring as he took in the quiet elegance of her grey suit and mauve blouse, the sleek fall of dark hair falling in soft waves from a central parting to her shoulders.

Jessica gave him a smile and took a small spoonful of chocolate mousse. It was rich and dark and delicious; she'd been working at it with tiny mouthfuls, savouring the flavour and knowing she'd never manage to eat all of it.

'Would you like some?' she asked Daniel, holding out her spoon to him.

'No thanks. I have to think of my waistline, you know.'

'I thought you were a jogger?'

'A faithful one—but it doesn't mean I eat desserts.'

'But you're not heavy,' she objected. Although stocky, Daniel was trim and athletic-looking, his wide face ruddy, his blue eyes bright beneath dark eyebrows, his hair still thick despite its silvery colour.

'Thanks to abstinence,' he groaned, sipping at his coffee.

'Well, I'm going to have to abstain in a minute. This mousse is obscene.'

Daniel put down his cup. 'Have you given any thought to the future, Jess?'

She glanced up at him. 'You mean another book?'

'No.' He waved the idea aside with a flick of his wrist, his cufflinks catching the gleam of the candles in their smooth, gold surfaces. 'Your personal future.'

'By which you mean Philip.'

He gave her a level look. 'Precisely.'

Jessica took another spoonful of mousse. 'It's up in the air,' she said casually. 'He's got another cast now and can get around more easily. I think the physiotherapy is doing him a world of good.'

'It sounds like he'll soon be self-sufficient.'

Daniel was giving her a route into evasion and Jessica took it with relief. 'I think he will,' she said agreeably. She wasn't capable of being introspective at the moment; her emotions were far too raw, vulnerable and confused for examination.

'And he'll be leaving?'

She shrugged. 'Possibly.'

'What's he going to do for a living?'

'He hasn't said exactly, but I have a feeling that he's going to be involved in corporate work.' She'd caught hints of Philip's future career when they'd been in New York for the christening and during her parents' visit, and she suspected that he was going to work with Simon.

'So he won't be sponging off you?'

'Dan, he never did. He's been paying half the house expenses since he arrived.'

'Like a roommate, eh?'

She beamed at him, grateful that he'd followed the misleading path of crumbs she'd thrown his way. 'Exactly.'

Daniel watched her, his eyes quizzical, frowning slightly. Then he seemed to come to a decision and his frown eased, a smile coming over his lips. He reached for her hand across the table. 'Jess, *I've* been thinking about the future.'

Small warning bells went off in her head, and she stared down at her captive hand. 'Dan, I think that it's time to . . .'

'You mean a lot to me. I think you've always known that.'

Jessica swallowed uncomfortably.

'We've had a wonderful working relationship and we've become friends as well, but about two years ago, I realised that I loved you. Not as a daughter, an older version of Annie, but as a woman. I know that there's a twenty year difference in our ages, but I'm still healthy and vigorous and capable of taking care of you the way you should be taken care of.' He paused slightly and then, taking her bent head as a sign of silent agréement, he continued, 'The last time I proposed marriage was twenty-five years ago, but I think the same formula still applies. Will you marry me, Jess, and become my wife?'

The proposal was so courtly, so gentlemanly and so civilised that it made Jessica's throat ache with pity for him and she lifted her head slowly. 'Dan, I've become close to you and I respect you immensely, but . . .' The words were hard to say.

He smiled at her gently. 'You don't have to love me. I'm not asking for that right now; I think it will come with time.'

She was shaking her head slowly. 'I'm sorry but I couldn't marry you; it wouldn't be right.'

'You don't have to decide now.'

'It wouldn't work.' Jessica pulled her hand out of his.

Daniel leaned back in his chair, and he traced the rim of his coffee cup with a forefinger. 'Is it Philip?'

'No . . . yes . . . I don't know.' She shook her head in confusion.

There was a constrained silence between them as a waiter came to the table, removed the half-eaten mousse and refilled their cups of coffee. When he was gone, Daniel spoke again. 'What does Philip have that I don't, Jess? He's selfish, cold and hard. He doesn't understand the workings of your mind or the direction of your career. He never treasured you for the woman that you were or gave you room to develop to the woman you've become. You'd have everything with me; love, caring, tenderness . . .'

His voice trailed off and Jessica clenched her hands together under the table, wishing desperately that Daniel had never made the proposal and that she didn't have to hurt him this way. 'I don't know what it is,' she said slowly, 'but there's always been something between us.'

'Sexual attraction,' Daniel said and then, catching

sight of the sudden blush on Jessica's face, added bitterly, 'So that's it.'

'Dan, I . . .'

'Sex didn't help your marriage; it broke on other things, on incompatibility, on anger, on cruelty.'

'I didn't say I was going to marry Philip,' Jessica protested.

'Then why are you getting involved with him again? Jess, this man is poison for you. He's going to ruin your life all over again.' Daniel suddenly leaned forward and banged one fist down on the table so that the spoons jumped slightly and nearby diners glanced at them with curiosity. 'Even if you don't marry me, Jess, I still care about you. We're in business together and we're friends. I can't bear the thought of you being hurt by that bastard.'

'I don't think he can hurt me.'

'You've let him into your house, into your life and . . . into your bed. He's intruding into every corner of your existence. Of course, he can hurt you; he can make you miserable.'

'I've grown up since we were married. I'm stronger now.'

Daniel shook his head. 'You're being a fool.'

'I'm independent.'

'Your emotions are involved.'

'They're not. I went into this with my eyes wide open, and Philip has no hold on me at all. I'm a free woman.'

But Daniel kept shaking his head and sadness gave his mouth a downward curve. 'It's obvious to me,' he said, 'even if you can't see beyond your nose.'

Jessica flicked a strand of dark hair back off her shoulder. 'Dan, I'm in control; I really am.'

His voice was resigned; his face held pity. 'The hell you are, Jess. You're in love with him—you always have been!'

Love. Was she in love with Philip? Jessica pondered

Daniel's assertion as she drove him back, the car
weaving smoothly through busy downtown traffic. She
was driving north on Massachusetts Avenue, a street
known as Embassy Row for its number of stately and
magnificent embassies, but she barely noticed her
external surroundings as her mind focused on an
examination of internal feelings. The new tenderness
she felt for Philip—was that love? The sexual desire—
was that part and parcel of love or was it strictly a
physical attraction, a need after long abstinence for a
man?

Marriage had taught Jessica to mistrust her emotions;
she had once 'loved' Philip and then discovered that it
was merely a forerunner to hate. Even the desire she
had once felt for him had been submerged by her anger.
The truth was that Jessica didn't have a clue how she
felt about Philip nor was she sure of his feelings
towards her. He had said that he loved her, but she
couldn't discount the suspicion she had that his return
was more symbolic of a desire to prove something to
himself than of any love he felt for her. Certainly, his
cool turning away from her this morning made any
avowals of ardour more verbal than actual. And he'd
said nothing about the baby; nothing about his heart-
breaking willingness to end a life that belonged to both
of them, and Jessica knew that his callous decision
stood between them like a high barrier. Sex may have
changed the equation and altered the balance between
them, but their night together was only a tentative step
towards a new relationship. In a way, nothing had
really been solved.

Still, Jessica was inclined to sweep away her doubts
whenever the memories of their lovemaking came into
her mind; she had a trusting belief that the passion that
existed between them would erase every problem and
difficulty. The thought of the night she had spent in
Philip's arms made her mouth curve upward in an
unconscious, reminiscent smile, and she forgot about

the morning's encounter in a sudden eagerness to see
Philip again. As she turned off Massachusetts Avenue
towards the side street that she lived on, Jessica looked
ahead to walking into the house and finding Philip
there and waiting for her. He might be reading on the
sunporch or writing at her desk in the study. She knew
that his physiotherapy session would be over by
lunchtime and he usually spent the afternoons working.
They had developed a harmonious rhythm of living
together that still amazed Jessica when she remembered
the awkward and angry days of her marrriage. Then
they had been pulled in different directions by
conflicting desires and interests; now they seemed to fit
together smoothly, the motions of their days meshing
without friction or disagreement.

She imagined him bent over her desk, the sunlight
picking out the blue-black glints in his thick hair or
catching the lean planes of his face. She imagined him
seated on the sunporch, his blue-jeaned legs stretched
out in front of him, the fabric stretched across the
muscular width of his thighs, one foot still in its cast,
the other shod in a brown western boot with a squared-
off toe and a slight heel. He concentrated so fixedly
when he was reading that Jessica had been able to
watch him for minutes at a time, enjoying the incisive
curve of his mouth, the masculine shadow of beard on
his chin and the tender sweep of his dark lashes.

She wondered what he would say when he saw her;
she wondered how he would look. She was so caught up
in her wondering that she was into the house and
calling his name over and over again before the
answering silence hit her. He was not in the den, the
kitchen, the living room or his bedroom. There was no
sign of Philip anywhere in the house, and it was with a
heavy sense of shock and stunned disbelief that Jessica
realised he was gone.

CHAPTER NINE

His clothes were gone from the closet; his shirts had been taken out of the dresser drawers; his shaving equipment was gone from the bathroom cabinet. Jessica frantically ran through the rooms of the house, throwing open every door and searching for some sign, some clue, as to where he had gone and why. But the house held its secret well. She couldn't find one glimpse of Philip anywhere; not a note, not some item carelessly left behind, not even the books that he'd bought remained on the night table by his bed. It was as if he had never been there; living with her, eating at the table with her, sleeping in the bedroom upstairs and making love to her through that long, sweet night.

Jessica raced down the stairs, not caring that she tripped when the heel of her shoe caught in the rug on the foyer floor or that her suit was totally dishevelled or that her hair was in a wild black halo around her face. She threw open the front door and ran out into the yard, shading her eyes against the angling rays of the late afternoon sun and looking up and down the street, knowing quite well how futile her hope was that she might see Philip walking up the street with that limp that always made her throat ache. There was nothing in evidence but a truck turning the corner, a red tricycle abandoned on the sidewalk three houses down and the first azalea bush of the season in bloom, its delicate saffron blossoms so profuse that when the flowers finally fell, the season of their beauty brief but lovely, they would form a pale orange carpet against the grass.

'He's gone. Left about lunchtime.'

Jessica whirled around to find Mrs Stanford standing by the hedge, her wrinkled face shaded by a straw

coolie hat that had seen better days and her hands
covered in a pair of stained gardening gloves.

'A taxi came to get him,' Mrs Stanford continued. 'I
saw it out my living room window. He was carrying two
suitcases and a duffle bag.'

'Was . . . he alone?'

'Heavens, Jess, but you're a suspicious character.
Nope, there wasn't a soul around.' She paused and then
asked with a touch of malice, 'You think he's gone to
some other woman then?'

Jessica shrugged helplessly, so unhappy that she
didn't even attempt to hide her feelings from Mrs
Stanford's curious gaze, and took a deep, shuddering
breath. 'I don't know.'

Mrs Stanford nodded shrewdly and made a wouldn't-
you-know-it sound with her false teeth. 'It happened in
my day, you know. Did I ever tell you about the time I
caught Herbert kissing Mavis Griffith by the honeysuckle vine?'

Jessica shook her head and crossed her arms over her
chest in a seemingly vain effort to hold herself together.
She felt as if she might come apart; the misery and hurt
and confusion hopelessly whirling together and then
flying apart, each one tearing at the inside of her, at her
mind, at her heart, with razor sharp edges.

'That old honeysuckle vine didn't make it through
the war and the Griffiths moved out in 1938, but then
that was before your time, wasn't it?' Mrs Stanford
barely took a breath before continuing. 'Anyway, I was
out doing a bit of gardening when I caught sight of
Herbert in a clinch with my friend, Mavis. And it
wasn't some namby-pamby kind of clinch either—it was
a real, down-to-earth, he-man kiss. I tell you, Jess, I
didn't think Herbert had it in him. And I was mad! I
was hopping, fit-to-be-tied outraged. If I'd had a
shotgun, if I'd known how to shoot, I would have done
them both in; cold-blood, hot-blood, whatever. But . . .
since I couldn't do either, I marched myself back into

the house, put a cold wet washcloth over my face and retired for the afternoon saying I was indisposed. That's what we said in those days when we didn't want to face the world.'

Jessica tried to smile, tried to maintain a polite façade, but all she could think about were the things Philip had said to her, his mouth brushing softly against her ear, and the way his hands had touched her body, more knowing and skilful than ever. How could he have left her like this? With memories so pure and sweet that it took her breath away to remember them? She couldn't believe that their night together had meant nothing to him at all and, if he too had felt the force of their passion, then how, in God's name, had he been able to walk out on her, without a word or a loving sign?

'And I was so jealous the whites of my eyes turned green, I swear on the Bible,' Mrs Stanford continued in a dramatic and garrulous fashion, raising her right hand as if in mock-testimony. 'I'd already been married about ten years and I'd never guessed that Herbert so much as looked at another woman as tried to kiss her. It was a blow to my ego. But after a while, I settled down and started to think. It came to me that I'd taken Herbert for granted. He was a good breadwinner and a good father. Of course, I never thought about divorce or separation, that would have been a scandal. I just knew that I was going to have to work it out somehow and I did. I kept Herbert real busy, believe me.' She gave Jessica a meaningful look. 'And as for Mavis, well, I knew there wasn't much to her; she was just a flighty sort. Herbert, I told myself, was just feeling a trifle experimental.'

The pain cut so deep that Jessica straightened up, afraid that if she gave in to it, she would collapse in the front yard, in view of half-a-dozen neighbours and the driver of the Bell Laundry truck which was slowly moving up the street. 'I'm glad,' she said slowly, trying

not to let the pain escape through her voice, 'that it all
worked out for you.'

'Now, Jess, the point of all this is that you're not to
give up the minute a little adversity comes your way.'
Mrs Stanford waved a gardening spade in the air for
emphasis. 'And you've got to have enough gumption to
go after your man and get him back. Your parents
tended to hand things to you on a platter, and you've
become accustomed to having things your way, but
now's the time to step forward and take a grip on life.
Go after him, child. Don't just stand there!'

Jessica stifled the sob that was rising in her throat
and managed a very small, very minuscule smile.
'Maybe I don't want him back.'

Mrs Stanford threw her a disbelieving look. 'Now
that,' she declared with disgust, 'is pure hogwash.'

Jessica was never sure how she parted from Mrs
Stanford and made it back into the house, but she
found herself in the cool shade of her living room,
wringing her hands together and wondering what she
was going to do. It was incomprehensible to her that
Philip was gone. Oh, she knew that they had parted on
cool terms during the morning, but surely that small
conversation would not have caused Philip to leave. She
hadn't meant to be so ... so distracted and talkative,
but she had felt shy and uneasy after their intimacy the
night before. That wasn't an uncommon reaction, was
it? And she had meant to come back and tell Philip how
silly she had been, how adolescent and awkward, when
what she had really felt was such tenderness towards
him, such an outpouring of emotion that ...

Was it her writing? Had that been the catalyst that
triggered Philip's departure? Jessica sat down on the
couch and stared unseeing at a pleasant mountain scene
that her mother had painted during her 'art' phase. She
couldn't imagine that Philip would *mind* her writing;
she had been a student when they were married and the

hours she had spent studying hadn't bothered him in the least. But then ... there was a difference between a student and a bestselling author. Perhaps the sight of her sitting at her desk, so busily engaged, had underlined for him the state of their careers; hers on the way up, his at a dead end. Was it possible that Philip, so masculine and assured and strong, was *threatened* by her success? If only he had stayed, she would have explained that ...

Jessica buried her face in her hands, feeling the tears seep out between her fingers, and knew that she would spend sleepless nights tormenting herself with reasons and theories and hypotheses. Rehashing the past and agonising over what might-have-been were futile exercises that did nothing more than make her miserable. Philip had left without explanation, and her choices were really quite simple. She could try to forget that he had ever existed or, as Mrs Stanford had suggested, pull together some gumption and go looking for him. The trouble was that neither option seemed possible. Jessica knew she'd never forget him, and she didn't know if she wanted to go after him even if she knew where to start. Below the hurt and the misery, another emotion was beginning to rise within her. Anger at Philip, a deep, rich and strong anger, was making her sit up straighter, the tears drying in her eyes. Anger at him for treating her like a piece of dirt he could sweep under the carpet. Anger at him for abusing her hospitality and leaving without even as much as a thank you. Anger at him for his exploitation of her body, for using her as if she were a woman without a name, a woman he had picked up on the street for a one night stand, never to see again.

Jessica's rage would have built to immense proportions if the phone hadn't rung at that precise moment, and she lunged for it, all her anger immediately swept away by a sudden rush of desperate hope that it would be Philip calling her with some logical explanation, an obvious reason why ...

'Jess?' Ben Harley's voice boomed over the telephone, loud and purposeful.

'Yes . . . it's me.'

'How are you, darling?'

She swallowed and kept her voice on an even keel. 'Fine and you?'

'We're fine, doll. I just came in from fishing and your mother is cooking dinner. We're going to play bridge tonight with some people we met who live a few doors down.'

'That sounds nice.'

'I just called to see how you were doing.'

His voice was soothing, more soothing than anything she knew, and Jessica warmed to it. It brought back memories of Ben coming home from the office and saying hello to her in his special fashion. He'd put his briefcase down on the floor, pick her up as she raced towards him, and circle her in the air before bringing her face down for a kiss. 'How's my girl?' he would ask, and Jessica would always think up something bad so she could elicit his sympathy. 'I fell down and hurt my knee,' she would reply, and Ben would be dutifully worried and concerned, examining her bony knee and its unblemished skin. 'You're going to be just fine,' he would say, 'so come and give Daddy another kiss.' Of course, she complied, basking in the warmth of his attention and knowing that she, above all other little girls, had the best daddy in the world.

'*Lost Souls* has been sold to the Norwegians and the Japanese,' she began.

'Honey, that's wonderful.'

'And . . .' Could she really tell him that Philip had walked out on her after a night of love? 'I gave a talk in Georgetown to Professor Brady's graduate seminar.'

'And you were a hit, I bet.'

'Oh, Dad, they *liked* it.'

'Don't be so humble, baby. The world doesn't recognise humility.'

'One of the big think-tanks here in Washington would like me to be on their Board of Directors.'

'There—see. I told you to think big.' He enthused.

'Well, I never pretended that my books were academic.'

'It doesn't matter. Quality shows.'

She tried for a light-hearted laugh. 'How come I get the feeling that you're my biggest fan?'

'Because I am, sweetie. I'm behind you all the way.'

'And . . . let's see . . .' she faltered.

'Philip? How's he doing?'

'Oh . . . well . . . he's got a new cast so he can walk without crutches and drive a car.'

'And . . .?'

'Not much else,' she said lamely, knowing that she couldn't burden her father with Philip's desertion, although the hurt she had received was far more serious than any cut knee or bruised elbow of her childhood.

'I just want you to know that your mother and I think very highly of Philip.'

'I thought . . . I thought you were happy when I got the divorce.'

'Honey.' Ben's voice was deep and sincere. 'You were happy so we were happy for you. The marriage was rocky; we'd known that for a while, and I never wanted you to be trapped in a situation that made you miserable.'

'But I thought you were angry with Philip.'

'When?'

'After the miscarriage.'

'That was nature's way of correcting her mistakes, Jess. It wasn't Philip's fault although I was furious when I realised he'd left you that day. Still, when I learned the truth . . .'

'What truth?'

'Sweetie, you asked Philip to leave, didn't you?'

'It . . . was mutual.'

'Look, honey, the past is over and done with, and it's

morbid to dwell on the bad events forever. You're a young woman with your whole life ahead of you, and your mother and I would love to have some grandchildren.'

Jessica couldn't help the cry that came out of her. Part of her yearned to go back into her childhood where answers and solutions came easily, flowing out of the generous bounty of her father's love. 'I don't think Philip wants to marry me anymore, and ... I'm not sure that I want to marry him.'

In an earlier time, Ben would have caught the strain of crying in her voice and would have asked for explanations, comforted her and offered firm and positive advice. But now he refused to take sides. 'It's a decision that only you can make, Jess.'

'Philip has hurt me a lot,' she whispered, angling for her father's sympathy, seeking his compassion. *My knee, Daddy, I hurt my knee.*

'Relationships are difficult, honey, and people get hurt in them. What you have to decide is if you love him or not.'

'Dad . . .'

'Marry for love.' Ben gave a low laugh. 'Now, doesn't your old Dad sound romantic.'

Jessica took a deep breath. 'Very,' she said. 'You must be going senile.'

'Thatsa girl. Have some spirit and keep your chin up!'

'If it got any higher,' she said, forcing her voice to be light and casual, 'it would meet my nose.'

The mantle of adulthood was heavy and, as she hung up the phone, Jessica felt its weight and knew it was a burden she would carry forever. The very last connection with her childhood had been severed, that unseen but strong link between a daddy and his little girl. She had known during her parents' visit that she could no longer place her problems in the hands of her parents and expect immediate and perfect solutions, but she hadn't quite given up the belief that her father was the ultimate god in charge of her life. Now she understood that he had stepped down from his role, that he had heard her plea and denied it. The message quite clearly was that she was on her own—for life.

But she couldn't help mourning the old relationship—it had been so easy, so carefree, so very reliable. She'd rarely had to worry about her own decisions or live with unpleasant results. Ben had always helped her, and by virtue of his age and experience, she'd rarely been steered wrong. She'd gone to the right schools and won the right degrees. Even her writing had been at his instigation; she'd been a scribbler since childhood and Ben had recognised her talent early on. The only choice that Jessica had ever made for herself had been her marriage to Philip, and that had been a disaster.

When she looked back at her life, Jessica could see why she found it so hard to make a decision now whether to let Philip go scot-free or begin a search to find out where he was. She didn't trust herself; she didn't trust her emotions. She couldn't be sure that her feelings for Philip, a combination of sexual attraction and tenderness, added up to love at all. She tried to imagine how she would feel if she found out that Philip was with another woman as Mrs Stanford had suggested, and then she shrugged her shoulders. She didn't feel a thing, not one iota of jealousy. Trying to picture Philip in the arms of some anonymous woman was difficult—the image kept slipping away. The idea was too remote, too artificial, too impersonal. Jessica got up from the couch, ran her fingers through her hair and straightened the twisted seams of her skirt. Her anger was coming back in a reviving surge and she welcomed the strength it gave her. Let Philip go wherever the hell he wanted; she didn't care, she didn't give a damn, did she? She was perfectly happy with her own life just the way it had been before . . .

Then the thought came to her, unbidden and out of

the blue, and she trembled as she sat back down on the couch, her knees suddenly buckling under her as if someone had hit them from behind, her eyes wide with shock. Was it possible? Unconsciously, she clenched her hands together and held them between her breasts where they pressed against the bone so hard that she could feel the pressure on her heart. Not Nora—surely he wouldn't have left her for Nora Speers! She shook her head in violent and utter negation. *No!* The idea of it was insupportable, unbelievable, ridiculous. Philip had no connection with Nora other than an evening of whiskey and sympathy and spilling his guts out to an ear avid for gossip and rumour. Or had more occurred that night than Jessica had ever thought possible?

The notion, once introduced, now lodged with certainty, a thousand reasons rising to support it. Where else would Philip go? He had sub-let his apartment in New York, and Nora was really the only person he knew in Washington besides Jessica. He even knew where she lived; they both did, having seen Nora one day entering an apartment building while they stood at a light on Connecticut Ave. She supposed that he could go to Megan and Simon, but she was sure that he'd find more solace with Nora—she'd been with him once before in a moment of need; it was logical that he'd turn in that direction now, especially if . . . if that solace came in physical terms.

The thought made her curve in on herself, her head bending to her knees, her nails cutting into her palms until they broke the skin in bloody arcs. Jealousy, she discovered, was a black force that could make her shake as if she had a fever, and it came to her that she had been quite blind and very stupid. Wasn't that what Nora had been hinting at the day they'd met her in the bar? That Philip had come to her and she had comforted him—in the best way she knew how? The thought of it made Jessica feel suddenly very sick. Thinking about Philip and Nora in bed together, his hands on her body, his mouth at her lips, the caresses equal and identical to those he had so sweetly practised on her the night before, made sharp pains shoot at Jessica's temples. Imagining them entwined on a bed was like looking down into a dark vortex where pain, hurt and anguish swirled in a nightmarish mix.

Daniel's prophetic warning echoed ironically in her memory: *I can't bear the thought of you being hurt by that bastard,* he had said with a wisdom that came of age and experience, but Jessica had denied the possibility. Philip couldn't hurt her, she had told him. She was independent, free and in control of her life. She was also a liar and a hypocrite; she knew that now. Self-deception had run in her veins for so long that she no longer could distinguish between what was false and what was true. Hadn't she been blind to her parents' unhappy marriage? Hadn't she been ignorant of her own imperfections, her self-centred behaviour, her immature attitudes? She'd hated Philip for suggesting an abortion, but when she looked back upon her reasons for wanting a baby, Jessica was horrified at her own audacity and selfishness.

She'd been hurt and bewildered by his walking out, unwilling even then to acknowledge her own role in the destruction of their marriage. And after the miscarriage, when the doctor had told her that Philip was waiting to see her, she'd been vengeful and bitter. Jessica had pushed the memory of that act as far down as it could go, but she now remembered her triumphant refusal, her satisfaction in teaching Philip a lesson. Let him know, she had thought, how it feels to be turned away from a hospital door. Let him know the amused sympathy of the nurses and the rage that comes from rejection. Revenge had been sweeter than anything Jessica had ever experienced, but she hadn't known then that jealousy was a knife with a two-edged blade; it slashed one way at the thought of Philip and Nora making love and another way at the realisation that her actions must have driven Philip right into Nora's plump, eager arms.

And it came to her, with a certainty she'd never felt before, that her jealousy, powerful and utterly painful, was the other face of her love, the two emotions no more separate than the heads and tails of a coin, seemingly opposite, but rising out of the same core of silver, their façades bound and inseparable. From the moment she had seen him at that party years before, Philip had been a part of her, and she could no more tear him out of herself and survive than she could tear out her own beating heart. Without him, Jessica knew that she would forever be a shell, a husk of a woman, condemned to a life of empty isolation.

Go after him, Mrs Stanford had said. *Get a grip on your life*. Did she dare? Did she have the audacity to follow Philip to Nora Speers' and confront him? Jessica couldn't bear the thought of meeting Philip under Nora's clever, knowing eyes, but if she didn't go, if she didn't try to get him back, he would be lost to her forever. And she was the guilty party; she had been the one who had acted this morning as if nothing mattered to her but her writing. It was no wonder Philip had turned cool and aloof. Instead of the woman he had known the night before, he'd found an idle, nervous chatterer who was only interested in her latest project and her forthcoming lunch with Daniel. Jessica groaned at the memory, thinking how she must have sounded; callous, flip and utterly uninterested in what had happened between them. No wonder Philip had walked out on her; he had probably felt as if *she* had used *him*.

Jessica tried to call Nora first, but the number was unlisted, leaving her with no choice but to go after Philip in person. Wild horses wouldn't have been able to drag Jessica to Nora Speers' apartment after the man she loved, but guilt at her own actions was far more powerful. It made her pull a comb through her hair, pick up her purse and walk out the door. It got her into the car and down the street while dread and apprehension settled within her like a sour, indigestible lump. Her hands trembled on the wheel as she navigated through the rush-hour traffic down Connecticut Avenue, and her heart was beating in a frantic, racing rhythm, a pace that accelerated when she pulled into a side street beside Nora's building and got out of the car, steeling herself for the interview to come. She didn't know what she was going to say; she hadn't a clue how Philip would react when he saw her. All she knew was that she had to make amends, that she had to explain why she had acted the way she did. Jessica no longer even cared that her apologies would have to be made in the presence of Nora.

She had to buzz Nora's apartment to gain entry into the building, and the surprised squawk that came through the answering box when she spoke her name made a small frown of concern crease Jessica's forehead. Nora had sounded completely astonished at her arrival, but then perhaps neither she nor Philip had anticipated that Jessica would have enough nerve to follow him.

'Jess! To what do I owe this pleasant surprise?' Nora opened the door to her apartment, her eyebrows raised to questioning half-circles. She was dressed in a long, flowing robe of green velour with matching slippers, and her hair had been pulled back from her face with a red band. Her voice was thick from a cold, and she was carrying a box of tissues in her hand. 'Don't mind the germs,' she went on as Jessica walked past her, 'I don't think I'm contagious.'

Philip wasn't there. He wasn't in the minuscule living room, the dining niche, or the galley kitchen. Jessica could see right past the couch in to Nora's bedroom and he wasn't there either. In fact, the apartment looked very much as if Nora had been stuck in it for several days. The bed was unmade, the couch had several blankets and a pillow on it, the television was blaring and the kitchen sink was full of dishes. But Jessica barely noticed the mess; all she could think was that Philip wasn't there, he hadn't been there, he hadn't run to Nora after all. She stood in the hallway, not knowing whether to laugh or to cry, her sense of relief so pervasive that she felt light-headed as if she had drunk glasses and glasses of champagne.

'I . . . wondered if Philip was here.'

Nora sneezed as she closed the door. 'God forbid,' she said. 'I wouldn't let a man in past the security entrance. I'm not fit for human eyes.'

Jessica turned to look at her and saw, with a touch of pity, that Nora looked even older than her thirty-odd years. Without make-up, she appeared tired and ill, the circles under her eyes sagging into purplish bags, the lines between her mouth and nose etched in deep, weary grooves. She obviously hadn't washed her hair in days, and its usual glossy brown waves looked dark and dull.

'I'm sorry,' Jessica said, 'I didn't mean to bother you if you've been sick.'

'Oh, I'm bored to tears with my own company. Sit down, why don't you?'

So Jessica perched on the edge of a chair while Nora turned off the television and began to fold the blankets that were strewn over the couch. 'I wasn't expecting company,' she said apologetically.

'Don't clean up for me,' Jessica said. 'I can only stay for a second.'

'You thought Philip was here?' There was a hint of the old Nora in the words, a questioning glance, a malicious overtone.

'A . . . a telegram came for him,' Jessica lied, 'and it had to be answered right away. He . . . wasn't there when I came home and I couldn't think where he might have gone to so I thought I'd start with you. You weren't listed in the phone book and . . .' she wondered how lame her explanation sounded, 'and I decided to stop by.'

Nora threw her an appraising look. 'Sounds important.'

'Personal business.'

'Oh.' When she saw that Jessica wasn't about to give out any information about the telegram, Nora yawned and changed the subject. 'How are you and Philip doing? Planning to get married again?'

Although she was flying high on euphoria, Jessica knew better than to let it show. Her answer was cautious and noncommittal. 'Maybe.'

'I always thought you were a great pair, you know, the beautiful couple, the ultimate lovers. I couldn't believe it when I met Philip the night of your miscarriage. I told him it was all a mistake and he should try to get you back.'

'You did?'

Nora grabbed a tissue out of its box and sneezed again. 'Lousy flu,' she muttered. 'He was so miserable. Anyone could see that he was going to be wretched without you. But he was stubborn as usual. Fraser used to say that Philip ran on nerves, willpower and bull-headed stubbornness.'

'You were going to marry Fraser, weren't you?'

'Who knows?' Nora said with a weary shrug. 'The relationship was in its infancy and it was too early to tell. But don't mistake my meaning, I was devastated when he was killed. I thought my own life was going to be over, too. That's what Philip and I talked about that night, you know, your miscarriage and my broken heart.'

'Oh.' The euphoria expanded until Jessica felt as if she would burst. Philip and Nora had never been intimates or lovers. The suspicion had arisen out of her own sense of insecurity, her own jealousy, her own ridiculous paranoia. And she wondered how she could have ever felt so much anger and resentment against a woman like Nora. There was something about the apartment with its clutter and lack of care that suggested a woman who had no roots, no centre to her life, and she sensed that Nora's love of gossip and her malicious thriving on other peoples' lives, arose from an unhappiness with her own. Nora was no more dangerous to Jessica than a fly that buzzed too closely. She could sweep it away with her hand and forget that it had ever existed.

'You know what they say,' Nora went on, 'misery loves company. That was quite an evening, getting soused on booze and sad stories. I think we closed the bars that night, although I can't remember much past the fifth straight gin. I had such a hangover the next morning that my roommate almost put me into intensive care.'

Jessica no longer cared that it had been Nora who had blabbed the story of her miscarriage to the press. 'I guess Philip needed someone to talk to.'

Nora nodded, sniffed and grabbed another tissue. 'He was crazy about you. Always was and always has been. Never even made a play for me, not that I would have minded, you know. I was lonely and unhappy. But he didn't; he couldn't get his mind off you.'

The euphoria lasted just as long as it took Jessica to get into her car and wonder where she should go next. She had run out of ideas on where Philip might have gone in Washington, and she could only come to the conclusion that he'd flown back to New York after all. She turned on the ignition and directed the car back in the direction of her house, thinking as she did so that she could pack her bags and take the next shuttle to New York. It seemed logical to her that if Philip hadn't gone to Nora's he would have bunked in with Megan and Simon.

But her first sensation of relief vanished when she considered what Philip had done and what his absence had demanded of her. He had walked out on her, driving her so crazy with misery, unhappiness and horrible suspicions that she'd actually been willing to demean herself and visit a woman whom she thought had been his lover. A sudden, intense resentment came tumbling back on her, now that her worst suspicions had *not* been realised. She burned from the shame she might have suffered and her own appalling loss of control when she had discovered he was gone. She had acted like a mad-woman, tearing her hair with her fingers, her face covered with tears, her mind whirling like a dervish without rational thought or reason. She was thankful no one else had seen her in that position; with almost every shred of her sanity and dignity thrown to the winds.

As she turned into her driveway, Jessica came to a cold, hard and angry decision. She wasn't going to follow Philip to New York; she'd call the Thompsons and let them tell Philip that she knew where he was. She wasn't going to race around the country after a man who hadn't even had the decency to leave her a note. She might owe Philip an apology for her actions of the morning, but then he owed her one as well. His leaving without a word had been inhuman, cold-hearted and insensitive.

She opened the door to her house and stormed into it, heading for the telephone, her head held high with an angry dignity, her emotions colouring her cheeks a high pink and adding a determined gleam to her eye. But she had hardly stepped past the foyer when an angry voice stopped her dead in her tracks.

'An interesting lunch,' it sneered. 'Five long and intimate hours.'

CHAPTER TEN

JESSICA didn't even bother to favour Philip with a look. She took off her jacket, hung it, in the closet, walked over to the mirror that hung above the chest in the foyer and gave her face a cursory glance, noting that despite the afternoon's madness she looked quite normal. And she had no intention of correcting Philip's misconception that she hadn't been home since eleven-thirty that morning. It gave her the chance to recoup her dignity and act as if his leaving had meant nothing to her at all. 'It was,' she said coolly, 'a very pleasant lunch.'

'I bet.'

'And Daniel happens to be a very pleasant man.'

'How nice for you.'

Jessica turned and saw that Philip was sitting in the wing chair, dressed in a pair of jeans and a dark shirt, his healthy foot encased in a suede desert boot. His beige raincoat hung over one arm of the chair and two suitcases sat at his feet. He looked tired and drained, his dark hair tousled as if he'd run his fingers through the thick strands over and over again.

'Oh?' she asked with a wide-eyed, innocent glance. 'Were you planning to go somewhere?'

'I'm back actually.'

'Really?' She walked over to the couch and sat down on it, nonchalantly crossing her arms over her chest, not wanting Philip to see how tense she was or how her hands trembled when they weren't pressed against her arms.

'I was going to take the New York shuttle.'

'And?'

'I decided not to.'

She gave him a small smile. 'I've never known you to be so indecisive.'

The grey eyes narrowed. 'Of course, I didn't think you'd still be out. I didn't know that Gilbert held such attractions for you.'

'I'm *not* having an affair with him.'

'I've heard "it's strictly business" before.'

'Dan and I have never slept together.'

'Dan—how sweet.'

Jessica glared at him. 'It's a platonic relationship.'

'I don't think you're capable of *platonic* relationships.' He retaliated.

For a second, the air quivered with their mutual animosity and then Jessica spoke, very carefully and very slowly. 'Just what are you getting at?'

'Your sexual urges, baby. They're on the strong side—or haven't you noticed?'

Jessica hated it when he was crude and mocking, and she stood up, her back rigid, every muscle clenched with fury. 'You can keep your insinuations to yourself.'

The more tense she grew, the more relaxed Philip seemed to become. He lounged deeper into the cushion of the chair, his hands laced behind his head, his eyes amused. 'Are you trying to tell me that last night was the first time you've had sex since the divorce?' he asked, his tone casual.

'It's none of your business.' She spat the words at him.

'But I think it is.'

'Why?'

'Because I'm going to marry you—remember?'

Jessica shook her head vehemently. 'No!'

'Yes,' he insisted.

His stubbornness infuriated her even further. 'Why the hell should I marry you?' she asked.

Philip's voice was quiet; his eyes watchful. 'Because you love me.'

Jessica's reply was a disbelieving laugh.

'Because sex between us is a dance; because we don't make a move that's wrong or inappropriate,' he continued.

Jessica looked away from him. 'Marriage can't thrive on sex alone.'

Philip ignored her. 'Because you might be pregnant.'

He had, quite inadvertently, handed her a weapon, and one so powerful that Jessica stood in utter silence for a moment, weighing it in her mind, savouring its strength and wondering if she dared use it. Then the memory of the afternoon rose within her along with a surge of anger and resentment at the misery he had put her through, and the scales tipped in its favour. 'So?'

Philip leaned forward. 'You wanted a child,' he said.

'That was years ago.'

'You don't now?'

Jessica flipped a strand of dark hair over her shoulder. 'I'm a career woman now. I'm too busy to think about having children.'

Now Philip stood up, steadying himself on the arms of the chair, his balance on the injured foot still precarious. 'I don't believe you.'

They stood face to face across the coffee table; Philip leaning heavily against the chair, the relaxed pose gone, the skin white around his mouth and nose as if anger and tension had drained him, while Jessica now stood in a careless fashion, both hands nonchalantly in her pockets, one shoulder lifted in a careless shrug. 'I've changed,' she said.

'Not that much.'

'I told you—I'm independent now; I don't need a man.'

'If you're pregnant, then I'm the father.' Philip persisted.

'You didn't care before.'

His teeth clenched. 'I care now.'

'Too bad.'

'Are you saying that you won't marry me if you're pregnant?'

The moment of revenge was so heady that Jessica felt quite giddy. 'Oh, Philip,' she said with a light laugh. 'I wouldn't *have* the baby. I'd get an *abortion*.'

He lunged for her so quickly that Jessica almost didn't have a chance to get away. He took a quick step forward and reached for her across the table, his face set in fury, the look in his eyes murderous. But his cast hampered him, slowing him down to the point that Jessica was just able to step out of the way, her heart thumping in fright, her breath coming short as she moved to one side of the couch. Philip fell over the edge of the table, his body crashing down despite his attempt to grab on to the arm of the couch, and he landed face to the carpet, the noise of his falling loud in the quiet house. For the few seconds that he lay there, Jessica stood frozen in shock, staring in disbelief at the sight of him before her, his dark hair gleaming in the lamplight, his broad back in its blue shirt dark against the cream of the carpet, his hips against the legs of the still-shaking table. She had the feeling that her words had touched him mortally, had run him through the heart, their power strong enough to kill him.

Jessica wondered why she didn't feel more triumphant. Hadn't she done what she had always wanted to do? Hadn't she handed back to Philip all the cruel hurt he had imposed on her? She'd had a revenge fantasy for years, a dream in which she inflicted punishment on Philip in the same way that he'd punished her and then watched him suffer in torment. But the fantasy, now played out in reality, lacked the satisfaction Jessica had always thought it would bring. She felt suddenly empty; the victory hollow, the revenge meaningless. She took a hesitant step towards Philip with her hand outstretched.

'Get away from me!' His voice was muffled against the carpet.

She stopped short. 'Philip, I . . .' She wanted to say that she hadn't meant what she said; that she would never have an abortion; that any child that came out of their union was one that was precious to her, but her words failed on her lips as she stared down at him.

Philip's shoulders were shaking as if . . . as if he were crying and Jessica's eyes widened in disbelief. She took another step towards him and then leaned down. 'Philip? Philip, are you okay?'

He rolled away from her, his face averted, and brought himself to a sitting position, his back to her. 'Leave me alone.'

The words were harsh and clipped, but there was something about his hunched shoulders and the timbre of his voice that made Jessica take courage. She kneeled down behind him and, with her fingers, she reached around his bent head and touched the corner of one eye. 'You're crying,' she said softly, feeling the dampness on her fingertips. There was a silence as her fingers rested on the side of his face and then she began, 'I never thought . . .'

He turned to face her then, and she saw the ravages that crying had inflicted. Philip looked older, deep lines had been cut at his nose and mouth, his mouth was turned downwards in a harsh curve and tears wet the skin around his eyes, making the lines around them seem more prominent.

'You never thought, what?'

'You've never . . . I've never seen you . . .' Jessica stammered in her astonishment. How could she express her wonderment at his tears? In all the years that she had known him, Philip had never shown himself capable of remorse or regret.

'You didn't think grown men could cry?'

Jessica touched his cheekbone where a tear had left a salty trail. 'Not you,' she whispered.

'I've cried,' he said bitterly. 'More than you'll ever know.'

'When?' she asked softly.

'After you lost the baby; when I realised that you weren't going to let me back; after the divorce.'

'But if I'd known . . .'

'You didn't want to see me.'   –

'It was revenge for all the times you'd shut me away from you.'

He stared at her for a moment and then said, 'And you'd have an abortion now—for revenge?'

'I didn't mean it,' she cried, her hands reaching out to him in a beseeching fashion. 'I want to have your child. I've always wanted to.'

Philip caught her hands with his and gripped them tightly. 'I couldn't believe that you'd say that to me.'

'I was just trying to hurt you,' she admitted.

'For the time I wanted you to have an abortion?'

Jessica nodded, her mouth trembling. 'I hated you then.'

Philip pulled her to him, his arms coming around her waist. 'I despised myself for what I'd done to you, too,' he said sadly. 'You see, Jess, I couldn't face having a child. I was caught in the same bind that I'd be in if I admitted to myself that I loved you and treasured you above everything. Having a son or a daughter would have been the end of my racing career. I would have been afraid to drive and to take risks or, even worse, I was afraid that I'd still race but I'd kill myself because I wouldn't be able to concentrate knowing that a child was at home, a child that needed me as its father.'

'I couldn't believe that you wouldn't love a baby that was ours.'

His arms tightened around her. 'I was so vulnerable inside, so damn soft, Jess, that I loved it already, but I pushed the emotions down and away. I panicked; I could only imagine still another bind tying us together when I was already fighting my love for you. And then when you lost it . . .' his voice trailed off as if the memory still had the power to choke him, 'I couldn't forgive myself for having hurt the both of you.'

She bent her head on his shoulder, her forehead against the fabric of his shirt. 'You were so cruel,' she said, her tears starting again at the memory.

Philip touched her hair with his lips. 'I spent the night in misery, knowing that I was wrong, knowing that I'd treated you in an unforgivable fashion. I thought about racing and saw how unimportant it was compared to you and having a family and how damned stupid I'd been, keeping you at arm's length as if you didn't count. So I came back with flowers in my arms and hope in my heart that you'd forgive me and we could start again.'

Jessica lifted her head, her lashes bright with unshed tears. 'That night—you came back?'

'The apartment was empty and I thought you'd gone to your parents. That made me angry all over again, Jess. You'd done that so often, gone crying to them with sad tales about us.'

'I . . . I don't do that anymore.'

'No, your mother said that you'd changed and that you didn't lean on them so much.'

'My mother said that?'

'When I was in Florida telling them that I wanted you back. She also said that your father was beginning to understand that he'd kept you under his wing too long for your own good. You're right, Jess. You've grown up since the divorce—you're a woman now.'

Once he had called her a child, a whining clinging baby that had never given up her dependence on her parents. She had never forgotten those words because they had cut deeply into her own cherished self-image of being a wife and an adult. It had taken her years to understand that age alone wasn't an indication of maturity and that Philip had been right all along. Now, he had called her a woman, and Jessica felt a part of her ease, as if wounds were closing, as if with one word a healing process had begun. 'Philip, I . . .'

His eyes were damp again, the silver in them shimmering as he went back to his memories. 'I called your parents then and caught them just as they were leaving for the airport for New York. When I heard that you'd gone to the hospital, I went there, but you wouldn't let me in.'

'I'm sorry,' she whispered.

'So I cursed you, threw the flowers into the nearest trash bin and headed towards the nearest bar. I got stinking drunk that night, too drunk to see straight. If I hadn't met Nora, I might have gotten killed just trying to cross the street. By the time, I tried to reach you again, you'd flown home to Washington and Ben informed me that I was persona non grata as far as you were concerned. I couldn't blame you; I deserved every bit of your hatred and anger. When you filed for divorce, I knew it was over.'

They were sitting on the floor together now, Philip's back to the couch, Jessica curled in his arms, her head against his chest where she could hear the steady drumming of his heart. She felt as if she'd been through a war, a massive conflict of personalities that had been fought in the dark of a forest where the paths had been unknown and motives tangled and uncertain. Both she and Philip had emerged into the open at last, neither victorious but neither conquered either. She had finally learned that Philip could feel hurt, and love, and cry like any other man, but she'd discovered his vulnerabilities at the same time that she'd realised that her own actions had set back their reconciliation three years —three long years of unhappiness, suffering and loneliness. She wished with all her heart that she had been in the apartment when Philip returned, his arms full of flowers, ready to speak what he felt, but she hadn't; she'd been in a hospital bed, pain clutching at her body, her mind black with anger.

She sighed and Philip spoke, 'I'm sorry, Jess. I've said it before—but I'd give my right arm to go back in time and change it all.'

'What made you decide to come back after all those years?'

'I was furious at myself and angry at you for rejecting

me—that was my first reaction—but then I began to think about my actions and wonder why I was so intent on racing. I went to a psychiatrist for a year and learned about my death wish; it isn't the kind of thing a man admits to himself and I started to understand why I hadn't been able to relate to you. I still loved you, I knew that, but I had to learn to like myself. I had to get rid of the stigma that my parents had foisted on me—that I was unwanted and unloved. I never really believed that you could love me; in fact, I didn't think I was lovable at all.'

The thought of the hurt that Philip had been carrying within him all those years made a lump come to Jessica's throat.

Philip brushed back her hair from around her ear and, kissing the skin at her temple added, 'When I look back at my initial reaction when you said you were pregnant, I think that part of me was afraid that I wouldn't know how to be a good parent at all. I'd had such rotten examples to look to.'

'And when you'd figured this all out, you decided to come back?'

'I read *Lost Souls* and that convinced me that I had to see you again.'

Jessica turned slightly so she could look at his face. He looked weary as she supposed that she did, his mouth soft and gentle, the skin around his eyes tight and shiny from the tears he had shed. 'I didn't think that you'd notice.'

'I noticed,' he said, his voice grim. 'I knew that every case history was ours in a sense. I felt your compassion for those women, your sympathy with their distress and anguish. I knew that you felt battered and I knew that I had beaten you—not physically but in every other way possible.'

'I kept trying to understand what had gone wrong with us.'

'And then in *All's Fair*, I felt your anger. I had to

come back, Jess, I had to set the record straight. I never willingly left you and I regretted every moment that I hurt you.'

She gave him a trembling smile and touched his mouth with her fingers. 'I forgive you.'

Philip lifted her chin so their eyes met. 'Marry me,' he said.

'My second proposal today.' she replied.

His fingers tightened. 'Whose was the first?'

'Dan's.'

'And . . .?'

'I turned him down, of course.'

'You haven't slept with him, have you?'

She couldn't resist teasing him. 'Maybe.'

Warningly. 'Jess . . .'

'I told you—it's strictly platonic.'

He took the hand she was shaking in his face and bent his head to kiss her palm. 'What's this?' he asked, staring at the broken skin on its surface, the arcs of dried blood.

'Scars of jealousy,' she admitted.

'Jealousy?'

'I didn't stay out with Dan for five hours, I came home at two o'clock and found you were gone. I . . . thought you'd gone to Nora Speers' so I went to find you.'

Philip sat back and looked at her with an expression of astonishment. 'Nora Speers!'

Jessica gave a shameful shrug. 'I imagined that you'd been lovers.'

Philip shook his head in disbelief. 'And you went to her apartment to see if I was there?'

'It was stupid, I know, and once she started talking I realised how crazy I had been. But you left without a word, Philip, without even a note saying goodbye.'

The kiss he gave her was a soft brushing of his lips against hers. 'I'm sorry, darling. It was brutal of me to leave like that.'

'I thought that you'd gone to her this morning after I

acted so . . . so blasé about our night together. I wanted
to explain to you what had happened—that I hadn't
meant to be that way, Philip. It was just that I felt so
shy all of a sudden, seeing you standing there, knowing
what we'd done just hours before.'

Philip touched her cheek gently. 'And I thought you
were turning your back on me. I thought nothing else
mattered to you but your writing. You were so
involved in it and wrapped up in your project that it
seemed you had forgotten all about the night we
spent together. So I packed my bags and sat at
National Airport for four hours, letting one shuttle
take off after another. Then I decided that I was
giving up too easily and I had to find out if your
career meant more to you than I did.'

'Never,' Jessica vowed fervently. 'Never.'

'The next time I show up in the morning after a
wonderful night before, I want a kiss, woman,' he
growled. 'Do you understand?'

Jess nodded meekly.

'And no more three-martini lunches with other men.'

'I promise.'

'We are going to have a very normal, married life. You
are going to write and I'm going to take a nine to five job.'

'Are you going to work with Simon?'

'Corporate vice-president in an aerospace firm he's
bought in Maryland.'

'That will keep you busy.'

'I plan to be a family man first.'

'Philip, I haven't even said yes yet and you're already
planning children!'

'Well?'

'Well what?'

His hand slipped from her chin to her throat and he
encircled the slender column of her neck with his hand.
'Will you marry me?' he growled in mock-threat.

'Of course,' she said, putting her arms around his
neck and bringing her lips up to his. 'Of course, I will.'

The telephone rang just as they came into the house and Jessica rushed to pick up the receiver in the kitchen as Philip closed the front door. It was late October and had turned colder than usual. A gusty wind blew leaves off the trees and through the air. The ground looked as if a red and brown snowfall had occurred, the grass covered with the wide maple leaves and delicate dogwood ones that curled and dried as soon as they fell. Fall had come early to Washington, ending the summer heat spell and causing Philip to close up the porch, the chaise lounges put away in the basement, the cedar table turned on its side.

'Hello?'

'You sound breathless—did I get you out of bed?' Megan was laughing.

'At this hour! It's past lunch already.'

'Don't get offended. I know all about newlyweds.'

Philip helped Jessica wrestle out of her coat and she mouthed the words at him—it's Megan. 'That doesn't quite apply in our case.'

'I tried to call earlier.'

'We were on the Mall.'

'Sightseeing?'

'We wanted to climb the Monument.'

Megan's shocked voice could be heard into the far reaches of the kitchen and Philip grinned at her. 'The Monument! Are you two crazy?'

'Crazy? Us?'

'With his gippy leg and your protruding stomach, you must have been a sight!'

'Actually, they've closed the stairs and we had to take the elevator.'

Jessica could hear Megan's sigh of relief. 'I swear that marriage has addled your brains.'

'How are Simon and Sarah Jessalyn?' she asked as Philip stood behind her and put his arms around her, his hands resting on the swell of her pregnancy. They often stood that way, marvelling at the miracle within her, the motions of life, the sudden kick and punch, notifying them that the baby was alive and well. They'd been so afraid of another miscarriage although the doctor had assured them that there was no reason why Jessica shouldn't carry this baby to term.

'Simon is up to his ears in corporate alligators and Sarah Jessalyn is going to become a sister.'

'Meg! You didn't tell me you were trying to get pregnant again.'

'I wasn't—this one is going to be making an unplanned appearance. Leave it to Simon's mother.'

Jessica was confused. 'What does Simon's mother have to do with it?'

'She made me so crazy with all her talk one afternoon that I forgot . . .'

'Oh, Meg, you can't blame another baby on Mrs Thompson.'

'Sure I can.' Jessica could almost see Meg grinning. 'That's the agreement in our household—that I can complain all I want and Simon can ignore me all he pleases.'

'And that works?' Jessica asked dubiously.

'Yup. He doesn't have to listen and I get to vent my frustrations. At first, it didn't work but when I realised that I could blame his mother for everything that went wrong and he wouldn't say a word, I had it made. You have no idea the things that woman is capable of—bad plumbing, poor weather, Sarah Jessalyn's one year molars, lack of will power . . .'

Jessica was laughing. 'I get it,' she said.

'I'm calling to invite you up for Thanksgiving—you can use me as a case study of the semi-reluctant mother although very married mother—if you're not working too hard that is.'

'Pregnancy is slowing me down but I like writing about it. Let me check with Philip first.'

'Is he there?'

Jessica could feel Philip softly kissing her neck and

she gave a low laugh. 'Very.'

'Ooops—sounds intimate. Listen, call me back; I'll hold the order on the turkey. Talk to you soon.'

Jessica hung up the receiver and rotated in Philip's arms. 'You're inhibiting my phone calls,' she murmured.

'How nice.' His lips moved to the curve of her jaw and slid up to her earlobe.

'Want to go to New York for Thanksgiving? ... Philip, you're not paying any attention!'

'Why are you so sexy when you're pregnant?' He smiled down at her.

'You're a glutton for curves, that's why,' she replied, putting her arms around his waist and trying to bring him close to her. 'Damn—this baby is already coming between us.'

The hard planes of his face softened as he looked down into her rueful expression. 'I love you anyway.'

'You plural.'

'You plural,' he agreed, kissing her nose.

She slid into his arms sideways so that she could rest her cheek against his chest. 'That's good.'

'How about a snappy comeback?'

'Mmmm?'

'I don't give all this tender, loving care for nothing.'

'Do I have to say it?' she asked, giving him a mock-pout.

'You're damned right,' he growled.

She looked up at him, a teasing smile on her lips that died away when she saw the intensity in his silvery eyes. He needed the confirmation of her love; the painful memories of being an unwanted child and unhappy adolescent were hidden scars he would carry all his life. The death wish had, as far as she knew, been destroyed by their marriage; Philip hadn't had a nightmare since that night in April when they'd slept together again, but when he stirred in his sleep, she always awoke, her heart beating with fear.

That was part of her love; the underlying knowledge

of all the sadness they had known. But there was a new hope now, a caring marriage, and the child to come. Oh, they still fought and she still grew angry with a fury that was as passionate as any desire she felt for him, but Jessica was no longer afraid of conflict or arguments. She'd learned that jealousy was the other face of love and that all the emotions she had felt towards Philip; anger, hatred, despair and attraction, sprang from its source. Her first marriage had been a denial of such feelings; the second was an acceptance and a joy.

'I love you,' she said, her brown eyes soft and wide, and then added what had become a very private, very intimate joke between them. 'It's a miracle.'